Lead a Dead Horse to Water

Ed edged between the family and the fender to reach the trunk. With a slash of his penknife, the twine holding down the trunk lid flew apart and the lid rose.

All eyes riveted onto the trunk's contents. It wasn't the spare tire. It was the huddled, bloody form of Mark Torrence. Mom grabbed the kids and bolted to the front porch, but Dad stood planted to the spot.

"Friend a' yours?" he asked stiffly.

"Used to be," Ed replied, voice hoarse at the grotesque sight.

"Watcha got him in there for?"

"I wish I knew," replied Ed in a shocked breath.

Lead a Dead Horse to Water

by

Mickey Scheuring

Best Wishes,
Mickey Scheuring

Commonwealth Publications

A Commonwealth Publications Paperback
LEAD A DEAD HORSE TO WATER

This edition published 1996
by Commonwealth Publications
9764 - 45th Avenue,
Edmonton, AB, CANADA T6E 5C5
All rights reserved
Copyright © 1995 by Mickey Scheuring

ISBN: 1-55197-210-7

No part of this book may be reproduced or utilized in any form or by any means, electronic or mechanical, including photocopying, recording, or by any information storage and retrieval system, without permission in writing from the publisher.

This work is a novel and any similarity to actual persons or events is purely coincidental.

If you purchased this book without a cover, you should be aware that this book is stolen property. It was reported as "unsold and destroyed" to the publisher, and neither the author nor the publisher has received any payment for this "stripped book."

Printed in Canada

First, to my sister Penny. She never flagged in her faith in me, and second to my husband, Al, who never discouraged me even when I was.

Chapter 1

Ed Riley arrived at the Torrence Riding Stable just as the sun hauled itself over the trees on the far side of the Chenagwa River. It gilded the dew-edged fences, buildings and bushes like strands of bathtub bubbles. Ed had spent many hours over the years at the stable. He had grown from a skinny and awkward boy to a tall, lean young man adept at horsemanship. His dark brown eyes matched his hair and a perpetual tan made him the envy of his friends.

The riding stable, generally just called the farm, was located along Randall Road, its property lines bounded by that road on the south, the Chenagwa River on the east and a line of mounding hills, bare of trees, on the west.

Ed passed the shabby two-story farmhouse on the left where the Torrences lived, then a paddock on his right that faced a large parking area. Swinging to the right around the paddock, and driving the width of it, he then turned left to park behind the barn, a huge affair with a pair of sliding double doors in the front, and a towering peaked roof. A large crossbuck door was centered on the second floor, with a winch projecting outward above it for lifting hay up into the loft. Inside, two parallel rows of stalls with a cross alley connecting them had sawdust-coated dirt floors. One of the large boxstalls, immediately to the right of the entrance of aisle one, had been converted to a barn office. The rest of the stalls comfortably housed the horses used for the riding students. Like always, Ed drove to the rear of the building and parked his battered heap by the back door of the barn's second aisle.

As he stepped into the interior, Ben Gordon, another instructor at the stable, brushed by him. Small, with fine, freckled features and sandy-colored hair, Ben often surprised people with his physical strength. He was taciturn, unless someone abused the horses; then, look out.

"Hi, Ben. Seen Mark?" Ed asked. Mark Torrence, owner of the riding academy, was of medium height and muscular build, and wore his longish, sleek black hair in a club ponytail. Although his sharp facial features and slightly pitted skin presented an intimidating picture, his manners were polished and he charmed all the ladies. The men he associated with felt they were with a man who knew his way around. Mark, always looking for ways to increase business, gave a cut rate for early morning lessons, and Ed, a cub reporter of barely seven months for the local newspaper, Town Telegraph, needed to count every penny. Ed had been riding since he was fourteen years old. His father had died when Ed was thirteen, and afterward Ed had spent several months struggling through depression. His mother, Ruth Riley, concerned at her son's continuing withdrawal, enrolled him in riding lessons at the Torrence Riding Stable. Mark became a surrogate father for the unhappy boy. Even after Ed left for college, he always found time to visit Mark during school breaks, and one of the reasons Ed enjoyed working in his hometown was, even though it was small, with limited potential in his profession, he could continue riding at Torrences'.

"Nope," Ben briskly replied as he rapidly strode down the driveway.

"Thanks," said Ed to the empty space, wondering what Ben was running from, or to. It was way too early to be in a hurry.

Ed strolled between the stalls, occasionally stooping to pet one of the many barn cats. Some of the horses nickered hello, while others turned their backs. Not much different from people, thought Ed.

It was every student's responsibility to get his horse ready for the upcoming lesson. Sophie, Ed's school horse, lived in the second stall from the end on the right hand side of aisle two. In Ed's opinion she was one of the prettier horses in the stable. She was a bright bay with black mane and tail and all four of her legs were trimmed in black with no white socks marring the look. Usually her cronies were stabled on either side of her keeping her company, but she was lonely these days. Her closest girlfriends were in the nearby pastures getting fat on grass and nursing their foals, while she had to stay in the barn and work for a living.

"Morning, Sophie. How's my sweetie today?" Ed asked cheerfully. He liked Sophie in spite of her bad habits, such as cornering him with her rump whenever he tried to saddle her or filling her lungs with air as he tightened the girth. She made up for them by being pretty good natured, otherwise.

Today, she had more interesting things on her mind than her rider. Ed tugged at her halter to cross-tie her, but she stubbornly refused to cooperate. Her attention was fixed on something in the next stall.

"Probably some cat having kittens," Ed muttered as he struggled with her, but she tossed her head, yanking the tie line from his hand. "Dammit, Sophie," he cursed, then, moving to her side, he peered through the low light of the empty stall to see what had caught her attention.

It took a moment for Ed's eyes to adjust to the shadowed figure lying crumpled on its side, and although he was facing away from Ed, the identity was unmistakable. It was Mark Torrence, his instructor.

"Mark," he whispered. "Are you asleep?" He was surprised to find him loafing because Mark always seemed to be on the move no matter what the time of day. Ed walked around the aisles to enter the box where Mark lay and stepped closer for a better look.

"Mark," he whispered. "You okay?"

"Mark!" He spoke louder. "Rise and shine, it's time for my lesson."

There was no response from the recumbent figure.

Ed leaned forward and gently grasped Mark's shoulder but recoiled in horror as the body, sporting a silver-handled knife embedded in its midsection, slumped backwards. Sweating and nauseous, Ed, with rare presence of mind, carefully backed out of the stall, sliding the door shut with his elbows. He didn't want cats wandering in there, and more importantly, he absolutely didn't need the chief of police, Donald Wilson, jumping down his throat for screwing up a crime scene by damaging the evidence. Wilson was still furious about the time Ed sighted a late model car sitting in middle of a field and called it in. It was Ed's horrendous bad luck that Wilson found his own daughter and the local drug pusher, Joey Lorenzo, in the back seat stoned and naked when he and Ed arrived. According to the raging dialogue that immediately took place, Wilson hadn't seen her in her birthday suit since she was born. It was a front page story, but Wilson quietly pulled Ed to one side and explained how difficult it was to live in a small town when the police watched your every move. Ed would be amazed at how so many seemingly little things were illegal. He took the hint and let the story die.

All this rattled through Ed's mind as he carefully looked around, assuring himself it was safe in the aisle. He fled for the phone.

The barn office, located on the right by the front door in aisle one, doubled as the tack room and the walls were cluttered with saddles, bridles, pads and other paraphernalia. Ed shut the door behind him, and shoving aside bottles of liniment, brushes and cans of saddlesoap, he grabbed the desk phone. Who to dial first, the newspaper or the cops? He quickly weighed his options, being fired or being jailed. His budding professionalism prevailed and he dialed the Town Telegraph's private number for Chief Editor, Mac Logan.

"City desk. Logan speaking." Mac sounded and looked exactly how an opinionated, bullheaded editor should look: gruff voiced, balding head, bushy eyebrows over piercing eyes and a pug nose. He had been holding down the editor's job at the Town Telegraph for years and knew everyone who was anyone.

"Mac," Ed frantically whispered. "It's Riley." He wasn't surprised Logan answered the phone. He was pretty sure Mac slept under his desk at night.

"What do you want, Riley, and why are you whispering?" He sounded as though the floor had been extra hard that night.

"Mac," Ed rasped. "I'm at Torrence's stables."

"So what?" Exasperation flooded the phone line.

Ed lowered his voice another notch, nervous at being overheard. "I've got a murder here."

"Yeah, right. Just like the "deceased" old lady at the nursing home."

"Come on, Mac. She looked dead to me."

"C'mon, Riley, not again," Mac groaned. "You make better copy than the stories you write." Ed's zealous efforts to produce a story were commendable, but his list of false alarms was toting up, and as much as Mac seemed to like having the enthusiastic young man reporting for the Telegraph, Ed was becoming something of a pain.

"Mac, this is real. Mark Torrence is lying in a horsestall with a knife sticking out of him."

"Your imagination's on overtime again."

"Honest to God, Mac. The guy is dead." The grotesque reality of it had given Ed the shakes. He gripped the phone with sweaty hands.

"Then you better call Wilson next or he'll have your butt in a sling. And Riley," Mac continued.

"Yeah?" Ed muttered, feeling queasy.

"Get your facts straight!"

"Yessir," he replied miserably into an already dead phone.

Ed dialed again.

"Portledge Police Department. Officer Pollard speaking." Wayne Pollard, obese and often arrogant with his tiny slice of power, was one of the two deputies Chief Wilson had to help keep law and order in the small town. He didn't need more because the state police stepped in on all the major cases.

"Pollard, this is Riley," he whispered again.

"Who? Speak up."

"Riley, Ed Riley."

"Oh yeah, the jerk who fingered Wilson's kid," he said, with a harsh laugh.

"Come on, Pollard, she did it to herself," Ed whispered defensively.

Pollard laughed again.

"Listen, dammit! I'm calling to report a murder," Ed snapped, his voice starting to rise, along with his anger.

"A murder? Bull!" Where would you find a murder?" Like everyone else in town, Pollard had his share of laughs at Ed's expense.

Ed explained again, increasingly annoyed at the deputy's attitude.

"You sure Torrence is dead? Maybe he's just asleep like that old lady you helped out at the nursing home."

"Pollard!" Ed's whisper became shrill. "The guy is dead! He's got a huge knife sticking out of his gut!" By now Ed wanted to reach through the phone and strangle the fat cop.

In the background, Ed heard Pollard's chair come down with a heavy thud. "Okay, kid, you stick around. I'll report it to Chief Wilson."

Hands shaking, Ed clattered the slippery phone onto its cradle and edged to the door, twisted the knob and scanned the area. All clear. He crept down the aisle to the stall where he had left Mark and glanced up and down the aisle one more time just to be sure he was alone, then, his heart thumping like a pneumatic hammer against his chest wall, he looked into the dim stall.

Gone! Mark was gone! Wrong stall! It had to be the wrong stall! The specter of massive humiliation loomed, obliterating all fear, and it sent Ed racing up and down the aisles looking in every boxstall for a body. Where the hell was he! Not one contained Mark. He returned to the stall where Mark should have been, peered into its emptiness one more time, then slumped, defeated, against the wall.

"Where is he?" he groaned aloud.

"Where's who?" a soft voice answered.

Ed jerked upright, slamming his head against the boards. "Annie, don't sneak up on a person that way." He turned accusing eyes at Annie, an assistant riding instructor of two years at the farm. Even with the dead and missing Mark on his mind, Ed couldn't help but admire her irresistible anatomy, and today she had her honey blond hair in a French braid, a style that enhanced her classic features and always made Ed harebrained when she was near.

"I didn't sneak. An elephant couldn't make noise on these floors," she replied. "What's the matter with you? Who did you lose?" She leaned against the wall, arms crossed.

"I lost Mark. I left him in that stall not ten minutes ago, and now he's gone." An oppressive gloom enveloped him.

"Riley, you know Mark. In that space of time he could be at the river pasture. In fact, he told me yesterday he'd be going down there often today to check on the mares and foals."

"He's not there, Annie. He should be in that stall, dead as a doornail." Ed pointed in the empty stall's direction. "Somebody stabbed him in the gut with a silver-handled knife."

Annie smiled uncertainly. "This is another one of your goof-ups, isn't it?"

"No one ever forgets," Ed moaned.

"Show me a body," Annie demanded.

"I can't. Somebody took him while I was talking to the cops on the phone."

She rolled her eyes upward, saying, "Yet another chapter in the "Ed Riley Book of Screwups"."

Ed knew what was going to happen next. Wilson was going to arrive and there would be no corpse. This was worse, a whole lot worse, than the daughter and the old lady combined.

"Help me find him, Annie. Fast! Wilson will kill me if he thinks I dragged him out here for nothing."

Annie smiled in placating resignation. "Let's go look, then," and shook her head as she followed him.

Ed knew she had serious doubts about Mark's death, but he was profoundly grateful she agreed to help.

Together, they checked the stalls and grain room, then crawled up the ladder to the hay loft. The high ceilings and dim, gloomy atmosphere gave the impression of an enormous mausoleum. Annie looked around one end while Ed took the other, but they had barely started searching the irregularly stacked hay bales when they heard the crunch of tires on gravel. Chief Wilson had arrived.

Chapter 2

Chief Donald Wilson was a cop's cop. At first glance his lean, athletic build gave the impression of a young man, but the flinty squared-off features on his seamed face and a greying military crewcut were dead giveaways that he was bumping around in his fifties and making a good job of it.

"Whatcha think, boss? Think Riley's got a genuine corpse here? Bet he don't," Myron Longmeyer, Wilson's deputy said, his narrow face, thinning hair and undersized skinny frame a sharp contrast to his boss. He nervously shifted his weight from foot to foot in anticipation of his superior's confrontation with Ed.

"Let's just wait and see," replied Wilson. He glanced around and bellowed, "Riley, where are you?"

Ed swung open the loft door. "Up here."

Longmeyer, startled, grabbed the pistol's butt in his oversized gunbelt, but Wilson never moved except to swing his cool gaze up to the loft.

"What's wrong with you," squawked Longmeyer in an adenoidal pitch, "sneaking like that? Don't you have any brains?"

Ed grinned down at him. "Sorry." They both knew he didn't mean it.

Wilson, ignoring the exchange, asked calmly, "Where's Mark, Riley?"

"This way." Ed signaled for them to go on into the stall area. Oh God, this is the end, thought Ed as nervous sweat soaked his armpits. As he started down the ladder, Ed prayed Mark would be there. If not, he knew he'd be wolfishly devoured in Wilson's fury. He glanced up into the loft for Annie, but couldn't see or hear her. Where the hell is she, he wondered. I should think she'd get a big kick out of what's coming next.

The Chief shouted Ed's name, sending him skittering down the rungs in double step. Even though Ed had learned to face down all the other cops in Portledge since he had started working at the Telegraph, the inflexible, intimidating police chief still made him feel like a pain in the ass little kid.

"Listen, Chief, let me explain," Ed gabbled nervously as he joined Wilson and Longmeyer and led them to the crime scene.

"Explain what, boy? Don't you have a body for me to look at?" Wilson stopped in midstride and glared at Ed.

By now they had reached the still empty stall. Damn! "Well, sir, I did, but it disappeared. Mark was lying here when I talked to Pollard, but when I came back, he was gone." It's happening again, Ed thought miserably. I'm jerking Wilson around whether I want to or not, and there's absolutely nothing I can do about it.

Wilson sighed hard and rocked back on his heels. "Gone," he echoed in forced patience. "Are you sure he was ever really here?"

"Honest to God, Chief, I saw him, and touched his stone-cold body. He's dead." Ed's sincerity failed to convince Wilson, and he didn't miss the derisive grin on Longmeyer's face.

"I don't believe you for a minute, but I'll check everything anyway," replied the Chief. "Don't want you telling folks I'm not thorough."

The officers entered the stall and poked around the straw, shining a flashlight on it and on the rough wooden walls that surrounded the enclosure. The dust-laden cobwebs hanging in the upper corners provided a haunted house atmosphere to the investigation.

"This is a waste of time, boss," whined Longmeyer. "You know we aren't going to find Torrence dead. Riley's just messing with our heads."

"Myron," replied Wilson sternly, "wouldn't we look pretty silly if the man was dead and we didn't take the report seriously? Duty is duty. Now go examine the loft while I finish down here." The policemen methodically searched everywhere Ed and Annie previously had with the same result. Ed waited alone at Sophie's stall until both men returned.

The Chief stared hard at Ed, shook his head and growled, "Guys like you make police work twice as hard as it ought to be. There's no sign of any crime here. Dammit, Riley, I'm sick and tired of your false alarms and I should press charges against you, but it would be a big pain in the rear-end to push it through."

The old lady and the daughter again, thought Ed. A couple little mistakes and they never let a guy live it down. It wasn't his fault they gave that old woman electric shocks to start her heart. She shouldn't have slept so soundly.

"You must think we're a pack of idiots," sneered Longmeyer, shifting the holstered weight of the gun on his narrow hip. "What makes you think you can get away with wasting our valuable time like this?"

Ed ignored Longmeyer. "Chief, he was here. I swear to God." At that moment Annie arrived and Ed wondered where she had been.

Wilson turned to her. "Good morning, Annie."

"Good morning," she replied with a slight smile.

"Did you see Mark this morning?" he asked.

"No. I haven't seen him since yesterday evening." She rested a large manure shovel against the wall.

"And what were you and he doing at that time?"

"We were in the barn giving the horses a final check for the night. He was telling me what stalls he wanted readied soon. We're expecting some new horses in a few days."

"You clean these stalls?"

She nodded.

He pursed his lips and rocked forward on his toes, hands clasped behind his back, giving the impression he thought her work was less than genteel.

"Do you have a problem with that?" Annie snapped. "Women's jobs aren't just in the bedroom or kitchen, you know."

"Now, young lady," replied Wilson, "there's no need to be crude."

"The truth is crude," she said flatly as she grabbed the shovel, wheeled and strode around the corner.

"Do you want me to get her back here, Chief?" Longmeyer asked angrily. "She's got no business acting like that."

"No, let her go. I've ruffled her feathers enough. Besides, I don't think she knows anything about Riley's "murder"." He turned back to Ed, his face tightening into a stony frown. "Well, Riley, you've done it again. If you ever again get the itch to call me in on another crime...don't." He turned to his deputy. "Let's go, Myron. We'll check the pastures, talk to a few people, then go back to the office and write this one up."

With a sinking heart, Ed watched them leave. He didn't miss the nasty smile Longmeyer gave him as the two officers stepped out of the barn into the morning sunshine.

Ed leaned against the wall and ran his hand through his hair. Annie joined him.

"Where the heck were you? I thought you were going to help me," Ed asked angrily.

"Hey, I said I'd look for Mark, not get tangled up with "Board Man" and "Lizard Face"," Annie quickly retorted.

"Board Man"?" Ed repeated, with a puzzled smile.

"Yeah. Doesn't Wilson move like he has a plank strapped to his back?"

Ed laughed. That he does, and Myron definitely has reptilian relatives."

Ed sobered quickly though, as the vision of Mark's body entered his mind. "I don't think Wilson believed me, Annie."

"You make it mighty hard for anyone to believe you, Eddie. Every time you report a crime, there isn't one. What do you expect? Your "corpse" should be here any minute to give you a riding lesson, and I've got a lot of work to do, so I'll see you later." She hurried away to catch up on her neglected chores.

I finally turn up a genuine crime, and no one believes me, Ed moaned silently. Unfortunately, this is one time I'll be proven right. Whoever did this to Mark is not going to get away with it even if I have to turn over every hay bale on the property to find the rat who did it.

Determined to start his own investigation, Ed strode purposefully out of the barn, absently checked his watch, and was astonished that three hours had passed since he had found Mark. He was gratified it was only eight-thirty a.m. His writing deadline was one p.m., plenty of time. By press time he should at least have found Mark and have a good idea who killed him.

He considered the possible suspects. Marlena Torrence came immediately to mind, the once beautiful, but now bloated, grey-faced alcoholic wife of Mark. He didn't know why she drank, or why she and Mark were always fighting. Maybe they'd had their last big battle in the barn. Then there was Mark's head riding instructor, Ben Gordon. Ed had seen him go berserk at students that treated the horses badly. Maybe that fury got turned on Mark for some unknown reason. Since Ed had already seen Annie, and suffered through her skepticism about Mark, he crossed her off his list of suspects. Following her was the usual parade of hired help that came and went as fast as their enthusiasm for the hard work and low pay, and, of course, all the riding students of all ages and walks of life. Offhand, there didn't seem to be any other likely candidates. Quite a list. He decided to talk to Marlena.

When Ed first met her seven years ago, he was fourteen and she was thirty-something. She caused him to break out in a boiling case of lust. Back then she was one gorgeous woman, but now she looked a lot different after all those years of being a bottle baby. He walked down to the big house and knocked on the door.

"Marlena, are you in there?" Stupid question. He could hear her grating laughter. It was louder than the blaring T.V.

"What the hell do you want?" she screeched as she staggered to the door. She swung the screen open and leaned against the jam. "Oh, it's you," she jeered. Jet black, frizzy hair surrounded her swollen face, and her robe barely covered her curves, heavyweight versions of the ones that used to inspire Ed's lascivious teenage fantasies.

"Hi, Marlena. Have you seen Mark today?"

"Well, that's a dumb question," she slurred, and pushed her hair from her eyes. "I sleep with the man."

"But did you see him this morning?"

"No, he left before I woke up. What do you want with him?"

"I had a lesson scheduled with him, and he hasn't shown up. Thought you might know where he is."

She fished a pack of cigarettes from her pocket and lit one with clumsy fingers, replying, "Look around, honey, he's out there somewhere." Coyly, she continued, "On second thought, why don't you come on in, have a drink and wait?"

"Uh, no thanks. I've got to find Mark for my lesson and then get to work. You know how it goes, no work, no paycheck."

"Huh," she grunted drunkenly, and wobbled against the doorway. "I remember when you used to hang around making big calf eyes at me. Now here we are and you want to leave. Whatsa matter? No guts?" Her smile mocked him.

Nonplussed, Ed stared at her. She had always treated him like a kid. Suddenly it's cocktails at nine in the a.m. Maybe she knew Mark wouldn't barge in to interrupt anything, ever again. Suspect number one. This wasn't so hard. He hated to leave, but was leery of getting stuck in that house with her. If she backed him into a corner, he wasn't sure how he'd get out of it. Better an ungracious exit now than a fouled up encounter with a drunken murder suspect.

"Mark's probably in the barn wondering where I am. I'd better go."

She sneered at him, "Well, scamper along, teacher's pet, but I'll bet you have a long wait."

Ed froze to the spot. If this wasn't an admission of guilt, he'd eat Sophie's hoof parings. "What do you mean, a long wait?"

"You know Mark. Once he's off and running, he forgets about everyone else, me included," she added bitterly.

"Guess that makes you pretty mad, huh?"

"What do you think?" she replied, a sullen expression crossing her face. "Well, since you aren't coming in, little boy, you'd better be off. I'm missing my show," and she slammed the door in his face.

As Ed turned to walk up the driveway toward the barns, he could hear glass smashing.

He found Ben Gordon in the arena giving a riding lesson. He had a woman, mounted on Rita, circling the area at a spine-breaking trot. Rita craned her head around to stare at the arena gate and the lady was having a hard time keeping the horse in line. Ed smiled. That horse knew her way out of every gate on this farm. They should have named her Houdini.

"Hi, Ben, got a minute?"

Ben glanced Ed's way, "What do you want?" His face was set in harsh planes and his student kept glancing anxiously at him.

"Where's Mark this morning? Have you seen him?"

"Of course not. You just told those cops Mark was murdered, so how could I have seen him?" He turned back to his student and shouted, "Your heels, lower your heels."

Ed brightened. "Man, I'm glad somebody finally believes me. Neither Wilson or Annie does."

"Get real, Eddie," Ben shot back. "I don't believe you, either. It's just one more of your "Cry wolf" stories. Mark probably has a perfectly good reason for not making your crack of dawn lesson."

Ed gripped the fence with white-knuckled fingers. "I'm telling you, Ben, Mark has been killed with a knife, and I'm trying to find where the murderer hid his body. It disappeared from the stall I found him in."

Ben faked a yawn. "I'll be old and gray by then, napping in the sun in my rocking chair." He returned his attention to his student, who had slumped dejectedly in the saddle, and Rita slowed to a foot-dragging walk. "Mrs. Smith, boot that witch. Make her go!"

Mrs. Smith, galvanized into action by the sharp order, quickly had Rita at full tilt.

Ed stood quietly for a few minutes watching Ben badger his student, got disgusted and walked away. There wasn't anything else he could do at this point, and without Mark's body, no one else was going to do anything, either.

Who could have killed him? Ed couldn't picture Annie plunging a knife into a person, plus, she had no motive that he could see to commit such a grisly act. Ben was a possibility. He could be a real nasty guy sometimes. If he were angry enough, he might have the nerve. Marlena was a solid suspect. She and Mark had supplied endless amounts of gossip for everyone at the barn. It wouldn't have surprised Ed a bit if they'd had a lulu of a bash in that stall that morning, and she had canceled Mark's ticket for good.

His mind was going in circles. Now was a good time to sit down with Mac and thrash this out.

Chapter 3

The car Ed owned could be called a "handyman's special" if it were a house. He called it a mechanic's nightmare. Its sun-bleached blue paint had been pintoed with gray primer spots to foil the cancerous rust, the trunk was held shut with baling twine, and little things like doorlocks and wiperblades failed to work at strategic momements.

He slid into its dusty, cluttered interior and pulled away from the farm. As always, the ride home was pleasant. The spacious fields rolled away on either side of the road to the steep wooded hills. Dairy cattle grazed in sociable groups, curiously, all facing the same direction. And there were tidy homes and farms along the way. Occasionally, there was rundown dump, but its presence made one appreciate how nice the others were.

Ed was getting close to one particularly ramshackle place when a tire blew, forcing him to pull over. He stood with his hands jammed in his pockets, stared glumly at the tire and gave it a sharp kick. He hated to change tires, something he frequently had to do since he ran them until the cord showed. A screen door slammed on the shack-like farmhouse, and he turned to see a greasy-haired, skinny man wearing ratty bib overalls followed by a dumpy woman in a faded, food-spattered, shapeless dress. Three beanpole kids of various ages dressed in dirt-smeared jeans and soiled teeshirts scuffed along behind in the rutted driveway. Ed pasted on an ingratiating smile and turned to face them.

"Hello, folks," he greeted pleasantly.

The tattered man ambled up, spat on the round and eyeballed the tire. "Looks like you got a problem, fella." The family watched wordlessly.

"Yeah, I do," Ed replied and waited hopefully for an offer of help.

"Well, I guess I can give you a hand. Open the trunk, and let's get the gear out." Still mute, the family moved like a tight bunch of grapes to the rear of the car to observe the proceedings.

Ed edged between the family and the fender to reach the trunk. With a slash of his penknife, the twine holding down the trunk lid flew apart and the lid rose.

All eyes riveted onto the trunk's contents. It wasn't the spare tire. It was the huddled, bloody form of Mark Torrence. Mom grabbed the kids and bolted to the front porch, but Dad stood planted to the spot.

"Friend a' yours?" he asked stiffly.

"Used to be," Ed replied, his voice hoarse at the grotesque sight.

"Watcha got him in there for?"

"I wish I knew," replied Ed in a shocked breath.

Dad uprooted his feet from the ground and edged away from Ed and his bizarre baggage.

"Don't think you'll be needin' my help," he said nervously. "You look like a strong feller, and the wife wants me to, ah, fix somethin'. 'Scuse me." He double timed a retreat to the pack huddled on the porch.

Ed called out to them, "Call the cops. They'll need to see this."

Clumped together, the family entered the house. Ed could hear the kids arguing over which of them would make the phone call and the angry shout of the father to "get the hell away from the phone. I'm was making the call!"

Once again, Chief Wilson was to be Ed's morning companion, and it didn't take him long to arrive.

Wilson slowly exited his police cruiser, Longmeyer in tow, and approached Ed, who stood well away from his own car. "So tell me, Riley, did you get it right this time?"

"Take a look in the trunk, Chief, and you tell me," Ed replied, and strode alongside the policemen as they approached the car.

Without touching anything, they contemplated Mark, who stared back with vacant vision, pupils dilated.

"Well, Riley, for a change you were right, and it's too bad." Wilson turned to Longmeyer. "Call in the state police, Myron. This will be their responsibility now. Tell them to cordon off the barn at Torrences', too. They still may be able to find something there."

Ed spent the next three hours being grilled by the troopers and Wilson while watching the state evidence team comb his car for anything they could find. He was repeatedly asked to describe the still-missing murder weapon. The suspicious looks they gave him over its absence contributed to the rapidly expanding sweat rings on his shirt.

The trunk lid, bumper and interior were dusted for prints and some areas of the interior were vacuumed. Mark was carefully examined, photographed and finally removed from the trunk. The ambulance took him to the morgue for autopsy.

Ed, Longmeyer and Wilson watched as everyone but them left the scene. Ed had been warned not to leave town. No one had to tell him why.

Wilson faced Ed. "You're lucky they let you keep your car, Riley. Usually they impound any evidence relating to a crime."

"Guess they didn't think you or your car were important enough to hang onto," Longmeyer added, snidely.

"Blow it out your nose, Myron. They got all they needed. Now if you'll excuse me, I'm leaving," Ed said as he walked toward his car. "I've got a column to write." But the last thing Ed wanted to do was get into his vehicle after it had served as Mark's hearse.

As the two policemen sped off, Ed was still standing by his car door.

Chapter 4

While in journalism classes at college, Ed had imagined that a newspaper cityroom would be busy and exciting. It never occurred to him to check out a variety of professional newspaper offices. He assumed they were all like the one he worked in at school or those on television, but the Town Telegraph cured him of that fantasy. There, it was the complete opposite. Quiet and sedate, voices were never raised, and everyone was impeccably polite. It was boring as hell. The society page and obituaries were usually the hottest items in print, but they were generally old news by three o'clock press time, thanks to the small town grapevine.

He walked into the hushed room and sidestepped through a cluttered maze of desks and metal trash cans full of paperwads to reach his own perch by the corner window. He had thought he was being smart when he grabbed that desk on his first day. In time, he realized why everyone else had shunned it. The sun baked through the glass in the summer, melting plastics and browning papers left lying on its surface. And talk about infiltration. In winter the wind blew like frigid little hurricanes through the fissures around the glass and sill. An old-fashioned word, chilblains, frequently entered his head November through March as he flexed his fingers and rubbed his hands together, feeling empathy for Bob Cratchit. The only other free desk was by Mac's office and as comfortable as it might be compared to his current weather station, there was no way he wanted to be sitting that close to the boss.

He greeted Marge Hayes as he passed her. She was the paper's society columnist. All the social dirt was laundered through her and put into readable print. She was one of the most respected, and often feared, persons in town, which Ed found fascinating, because she was a mousey little woman who never said much, and seldom left her desk during working hours. It was said she had a grapevine on the county that resembled a fisherman's seining net.

"Hi, Riley," she replied. "Did you interview Mark's killer yet?"

"Did Mac mention Mark's death to you?" asked Ed.

"No," she replied, smiling like Mona Lisa.

Ed shook his head, wondering who her pipeline was this time. "I'm working on it," he answered.

He sat at his decrepit typewriter and rolled in a sheet of paper to begin his climb to fame and fortune. He wished he could climb with a computer, but Mac wouldn't have it. The old ways are the best ways, Mac always said. He wrote his editorials in longhand with a soft lead pencil. The secretary snarled with frustration when assigned to type it. The typesetters wouldn't accept it any other way, even from Mac. As Ed fiddled with the paper in the platen, Mac emerged from his office and approached Ed's desk.

His bald head gleamed under the fluorescent lights, but his bushy salt and pepper eyebrows more than made up for his empty pate. As he walked, he brushed cracker crumbs off his white shirt. He had recently substituted saltines for cigarettes.

"So, Riley," he growled. "What's going on with Mark Torrence? Is he really dead?"

"Yeah, he's dead all right. I've never seen anything like it." Ed had been trying to blot the grotesque sight of Mark from his mind, but the image kept flashing like a dirty slide show at a drunken fraternity party.

Mac leaned against the desk, his voice softening a shade. "It's too bad your friend died, Eddie. Is there anything I can do?"

Ed wanted badly to be the exclusive reporter for the Torrence story. The better ones were always handled by Ted Russell, who'd been with the paper since dirt was new and was the only street reporter until Ed was hired. He decided it couldn't hurt to ask.

"Give me the story exclusively with no interference from Ted. Finding Mark's body and being his student has given me a unique perspective," Ed observed, sourly. "Besides, it'll help me do one last thing for Mark." He thought of the offhand fatherly guidance Mark had given him over the years, advise with no preaching.

"You put me in a tough spot, Ed. This is the best story of the year. Ted will howl if I give it to you." He tapped his foot and hummed off key while he thought it over. "Give me something in writing today. If I like it, you can have the piece."

Ed grinned in relief. "Boss, you won't regret it. It'll be the best story you've ever read."

"I kind of doubt that, but go ahead. And Riley, if it stinks, it's back to "human interest" for you." Mac removed his bulk from Ed's desk and returned to his office.

Ed started tapping furiously on the typewriter keys. He rattled away the hour on the ancient instrument, occasionally checking his thesaurus and dictionary, frequently dabbing the paper with whiteout until, finally, he yanked the page from the machine. He nodded his head at it, a satisfied smile on his face, and turned it over to Mac.

His beefy boss leaned back in his chair, Eddie's wrinkled article in hand, and slowly read it.

Ed leaned against the doorframe of Mac's office, seemingly nonchalant, but the agitated bounce of Ed's leg told on him.

"Well, Ed," Mac said as he smoothed out the paper that was embossed with Ed's ambition, "this will be fine. I'll take it from here, and you go buy yourself a congratulatory beverage." He waved Ed from the office.

Ed's face split in two, a smiling upper, and a laughing lower, half. For a short time he forgot the reason for the article, and enjoyed only the fruits of it. A Byline. The goal of any reporter worth his press pass. He headed for Red's Place, a local bar. As he trotted happily down the outside steps of the newspaper building, he encountered Officers Pollard and Longmeyer. Smiling conspiratorially at each other, they stopped Ed.

"My, my, look who we have here," said Longmeyer in derision. "The owner of the town's newest meatwagon. What do we need with an ambulance when we've got Riley's car trunk, hey Pollard?"

Pollard laughed and added, "Nice ride you gave Torrence, Eddie. Did you offer it before or after you killed him?"

"Knock it off. You know I didn't kill Mark." Ed was furious.

"Yeah, probably not," agreed Longmeyer, curling his lip. "No spine."

"No Spine, huh? I'll tell you what. Whoever did this to Mark is going to be sorry. I'll keep this story alive no matter how long it takes to find his murderer. In fact, my first article will be in today's paper, and they won't stop until they catch the guy and throw a rope over a hanging tree."

"Is that so," replied Pollard. "Bet it ends up on a back page in two weeks and falls right off the paper before the month's out. People lose interest, you know."

"Not this time. This is the front page until the creep is in the slammer for good," Ed said firmly.

"Very diligent of you," Longmeyer mocked. "By the way, Wilson and I told Marlena what happened. She flipped out. It was a good thing that babe, Annie, was there. Otherwise, I think we'd be putting the widow in the ground too."

Ed frowned at him. "You're just a bundle of compassion, aren't you, Myron? How did Annie take it?"

"That broad is an iceberg. She hardly blinked when Wilson told them. She just said, 'For once Eddie was right, damn it.' Kinda funny, don't you think? You can bet we'll be checking her out." Longmeyer smirked at Ed.

"Just leave her alone, Myron. Annie's no more guilty of the crime than I am!" Ed shouted. "In fact, she going to help me solve this case before you stumblebums do," he added, and immediately wondered where that fantasy came from. His job was to report, not investigate, this story, and Annie would probably shoot him for what he had just said.

Pollard looked at Ed fiercely and ordered, "Don't you be interfering in a crime investigation, sonny, or you'll be reporting what life is like in a jail cell. C'mon Myron, we've wasted enough time with this pup."

Ed fumed as he watched the policemen walk away. You think Annie and I couldn't solve this murder? Well, think again. Maybe I'll try just to jerk you around, though I don't know that Annie would be interested. Red's Place forgotten, Ed ran back up the steps into the building and into the production area of the newspaper. He anxiously watched as the crew created the mockup of the front page with his story headlined "RIDING TEACHER MURDERED." A former publicity photo of Mark on one of his favorite horses occupied a three inch by five inch space directly above Ed's report. The photo and story were boxed in a thick black line. Wow, thought Ed. You'd think the President of the U.S.A. had died.

"This looks great," he commented to Jerry, the layout man.

"Nothing but the best for a grisly crime," Jerry responded lightly. "Papers sell like crazy with this kind of stuff. We'll be printing extra editions today."

Ed checked out his story over Jerry's shoulder. It was minus the furious editing his reports usually got. Now the whole town would know he was a great reporter. For the rest of the afternoon Ed followed the progress of his story from mockup to printing as eagerly as a kid watching his mother baking a batch of chocolate chip cookies.

The production people, knowing it was Ed's first big story, were patient with him as they prepared the layout pages prior to printing the newssheet.

As the pages went to press, Ed sat at the last printing press waiting for the finished product. It emerged promptly at two forty-five p.m. He grabbed the first edition as they stacked into piles for distribution.

"Yes!" he said exultantly. The elation of owning a headline, any headline, blotted out the cause. It was his finest moment, to date.

"Way to go," said Jerry, as he, too, read the edition. "Take it home, Ed. Paste it on the wall. Not many people get great headlines in a lifetime of reporting, not even Ted Russell."

"No kidding? Ted never had a headline?" Ed asked, surprised.

"Well, yeah, he's had headlines, but they were all political or local town business. Nothing like this." Jerry slapped Ed on the back.

Ed grinned in appreciation of Jerry's admiration, but even more, he was delighted he had beaten out the insufferable Russell in their mutual profession. After receiving good-natured congratulations from the others in the press room, Ed floated to the local chromexplated diner for supper. While dining on his favorite, lasagna, he re-read the front page, followed up by the rest of the paper. A few people stopped at his table to comment on the crime and his coverage. A dose of nuclear radiation couldn't have made him glow any brighter. Even having to cover the Sewer Commission meeting that evening didn't dampen his spirits.

It was a curious day, he reflected, as he drifted off to sleep. The terrible loss of a friend enhanced his own sorry reputation. Weird.

Chapter 5

Ed stood on the courthouse steps high above the cheering crowd that spread out over the sidewalks and grass, clear to the street, thirty yards away. "Eddie, Eddie," they chanted. Joyful and boisterous, they showered him with accolades. He waved and called out to them, "Thank you, thank you. You're a great bunch of readers of the "Telegraph."

There was only one jarring note. Someone kept poking him in the ribs. Irritated, Ed turned and a flashlight beam flooded his eyes, blinding him.

"Get out of bed, creep," the rib poker hissed, "and no fast moves."

The cheering crowd abruptly disappeared as Ed, wide awake and petrified, slid slowly and cautiously out of bed, his eyes glued on the pistol in the intruder's gloved hand. The dull gleam of the metal, highlighted by the flashlight, made Ed think of oily puddles in dark alleys, places where bodies from unexplained deaths were found. He felt his stomach lurch, greasily, into his throat.

"What do you want?" Ed asked in a choked voice.

"Listen, creep. I don't want you snooping around Torrence's farm no more. You got your little story and now it's finished. Lay off."

A trickle of indignation watered down Ed's fear. "This story is only beginning, Bud. Who the hell are you to interfere with the free press?"

Suddenly, the flashlight aimed toward the ceiling as the man tucked it under his arm. He yanked Ed close to him by his teeshirt, slamming the pistol against Ed's head. Ed sagged slightly, more from fear than injury.

"Look, you jerk," snarled the intruder, the odors of stale cigarettes and beer rolling off him. "Don't smart off to me. I don't want you snooping around no more. You got that?"

The sweat poured down Ed's face, around the tip of the pistol barrel now dug into his cheek, and dripped on the man's shirt. Angry dark eyes, visible over the yellow striped handkerchief the man wore as a mask, reflected from the light of the flashlight and bored into Ed, who nodded wordlessly. The gun against his face had turned his tongue into cement.

The stranger spun Ed away from him. "Turn around and spread your arms up the wall. Don't move for ten minutes, and don't call no cops. Got it?"

"Yeah. I got it," Ed croaked and an instant after he assumed the ordered position, his gentleman visitor walloped Ed in the back of the head with the butt of his pistol.

Ed oozed back to the surface of the world after twenty minutes, he later estimated, in a black tar pit. He felt the back of his head as gently as possible, but all the care in the world couldn't have stopped the shaft of pain that sheared through to his eyeballs and the touch of his fingers. It took a few minutes for his mental functions to return. Expecting the intruder to attack his head again and browbeat him with double-negatives, he crawled slowly onto his bed, slumped softly down, turned on the small bedside light, and reached for the phone to dial Mac at home.

"Mac?" Ed whispered. He nervously glanced through the doorway into the kitchen/livingroom area, wincing in pain at the movement. It was too dark to see much, but he looked anyway. He examined his hand for blood from his head and was relieved to see none.

"Who is this?" muttered a sleepy voice.

"Mac, it's me, Riley. You're not gonna believe what just happened!" Ed clutched the phone in a strangler's grip, careful not to touch his ear with it.

"Riley, again?" he responded thickly. "Oh, brother. Where what just happened?"

"At my place! In my bedroom!"

"I don't want to hear about your bedroom exploits, especially at, what, three in the morning?"

"No, Mac, that's not it. A guy broke in here and cracked my skull...with a gun!" Ed could hear Mac's bedsprings squeaking as he struggled to sit up.

"Tell me the rest!" he barked.

Haltingly, Ed took a couple of minutes to tell his tale. As he talked, he struggled slowly into his jeans and a fresh teeshirt. He excused himself briefly to carefully ease the shirt over the now egg-sized swelling on the back of his head.

At the story's end Mac sighed, "Well, Riley, you're in it now. You were always complaining that nothing ever happens in this town, and now you've got it coming out of your ears."

"I think my brains are coming out of my ears. That guy did a number on me, but there's not a chance I'll give up on this story. I owe it to Mark."

"Atta boy," congratulated Mac. "Papers would

be full of recipes and comics if we let goons intimidate us. You better call Wilson now and maybe get your head x-rayed, and if you check out okay you get right on it. I liked your piece, and the story is still yours."

"Thanks, Mac. You won't regret it."

"Just watch your butt, kid. Things are getting a little hot."

Ed hung up the phone and felt a pang of guilt. Climbing to the top was great, but getting there over Mark's body was damned ghoulish. But this was his big chance and he wasn't going to blow it. He hoped that if Mark could materialize and talk, he'd tell Ed to hack out a hundred columns if it would help find his murderer.

Ed dialed again. Wilson picked up on the other end, which surprised Ed. He wondered if the Chief ever slept.

"Chief, this is Ed Riley. I hate to bother you, but a guy was just in my apartment threatening me about being too enthusiastic about covering the Torrence story." He could hear an exasperated sigh over the line.

"Riley, are you hurt?"

"Kinda. The jerk knocked me cold when my back was turned," Ed replied. "I've got a egg on the back of my head geese would fight over. Guess I'll live, though."

"You better get to the hospital for x-rays. Can you make it on your own, or do you need a ride?"

After a brief argument about the state of Ed's health and ability to drive, Wilson said he'd be right over. Ed met him on the front step, not caring to have the policeman pass judgement on the condition of his apartment.

"Too bad you came out, Riley. Now, we have to go back in so I can examine for evidence."

"There's not going to be any real evidence," Ed replied. "The guy wore gloves and used a .22 caliber pistol. I don't think looking the place over would accomplish anything. I just wanted you to know about it right away."

"Tell you what," Wilson said. "We'll check your apartment in the morning. Just don't touch anything you think he did."

"Fine by me," agreed Ed.

They spent the next hour at the hospital only to find out Ed had an iron cranium and it would take more than the butt of a .22 to crack it.

"That's quite a nice swelling you've got, young man," Dr. Edders commented cheerfully as he finished wrapping Ed's head. "Now don't be aggravating the nice criminals anymore." The bustling, happy physician laughed at his little joke. "Here's an ice-pack to take with you."

Ed gingerly placed the ice against the throbbing egg and promptly removed it again. "Jeeze, that hurts worse than the injury."

"Just give it a minute. It'll numb that swelling and shrink it a bit." Dr. Edders escorted Ed back to Chief Wilson. "Here's our young man, Officer. No sign of fracture. He should be just fine in a few days."

Ed tossed the ice-pack into the trash outside the emergency door and joined Wilson in the police cruiser. "How come you gave me a ride here tonight? Don't they have ambulances for that sort of thing?"

Wilson glanced over at Ed. "For one thing, you'd never go if I didn't take you, and if you did go the hospital by yourself, probably something would happen to you on your way. You're a trouble magnet."

Wilson had no sooner spoken the words when

the radio crackled to life. "See the man. 10-49 Code 5, Code 30. All available vehicles."

The Chief picked up his transmitter and answered, "Unit 1, 10-4, on my way." He then turned to Ed and said, "You see? Just being near you attracts trouble." But he grinned slightly after he said it.

"What's going on?" Ed was excited. He knew the codes the cops used and this particular batch meant they were going to a stakeout that was panning out, big time.

"I don't have time to take you home, so you may as well know what you're in for. An organized bunch called the Posse Comitatus has been camped at the old Miller farm for the past few months. The authorities think they've been stashing assault weapons and dealing drugs. Apparently, the state boys are making their move tonight and want every cop in the county there, including the town police."

"What can you do?" Ed asked. He knew Wilson's authority only extended to the city limits.

"Moral support, I guess," Wilson replied. "Get your pad and pencil ready. There might be some real action."

Fortunately, Ed did have the tools of the trade with him. Always having them on hand, no matter what, had been ingrained by school and Mac.

They barreled down Randall Road, past Torrences' three miles or so, and turned down a rutted road that led to the shabby farmhouse, collapsing barns and shrubbed-in fields of the former Miller "estate." The house and outbuildings were already surrounded by police cars from the state and county. Wilson's vehicle was the first from a nearby town, but as Ed looked back he could see that Pollard was right behind them. Despite his thumping goose egg headache, Ed jumped out of the car and waded through the tall grass, skirting the rusting farm implements, and approached the state police only to feel the clamp of a hand on his shoulder.

"Hold on, Eddie," ordered Wilson. "You stay behind me, not in front."

Ed felt a flush of irritation, but waited for the Chief to lead rather than jeopardize the strange camaraderie that the man was allowing. Maybe, thought Ed, Wilson is Mr. Hyde by day and Dr. Jekyll by night. The three of them walked to the rear of the police line together.

Pollard whispered to Ed, "Wilson must be desperate for company tonight, huh?" and laughed softly.

Ed ignored him as they mingled with the other police.

Cruiser headlights bathed the house, and the people within shouted vulgarities out the windows. The spokesman for the troopers held a bullhorn up and ordered, apparently not for the first time, the occupants of the house to come out and read them their Miranda rights, en masse, through the horn. Suddenly, shots from the house rang out, causing everyone outside to crouch down behind any available car, tree or piece of rusty farm machinery.

Ed whispered to Pollard, who was having a very hard time at the squat, "Who are these people? What's the Posse, anyway?"

Pollard, sweating in the cool night air, answered breathlessly, "Fringe bunch. Won't pay taxes; don't answer to the federal government; county cops are the only law they recognize. They got their own view on how this county should be run, and some of them go hog wild with it."

"Like this bunch," Ed added.

"Yeah. These guys are real loose cannons. We've been keeping an eye on them for a while now. I guess the bigwigs are in there tonight, or the state boys wouldn't have had this raid."

Ed scribbled rapidly in his notebook as Pollard talked and the pistol and shotgun blasts punctuated his sentences with jerky letters. The pen in his hand was slippery with nervous sweat, a general body affliction he was currently sharing with Pollard.

An occasional yelp of pain could be heard from the house when a bullet found a new home, and finally someone inside yelled, "Enough, we've had enough. We're coming out."

The five men and two women who straggled out the door were a revelation to Ed. One of the men was Jim Brown, a mechanic from a garage in town, and a woman he recognized had served him coffee at the donut shop plenty of times. Her name was Emily. At least that's what the tag on her uniform had written on it.

As the troopers cuffed the group, Ed sped from one prisoner to another trying to get their names and addresses and any other information he could scrounge from them in the confusion. Unfortunately for him, they had all been well trained at what to do in case of arrest and Ed came up pretty much empty-handed. Except for Emily. She offered him a "good time" if he would stand her bail. The trooper turned Ed away and firmly tucked her into the car.

Several ambulances arrived and the paramedics entered the house under police escort to attend the wounded inside. Ed tried to join them.

A rock-jawed state trooper stopped him at the steps. "What the heck are you doing, coming across the police line, mister? Who are you with?"

"I'm with Chief of Police Wilson," Ed replied with bravado, hoping to snow this guy enough to get inside. The most he managed was a peek around the trooper through the front door, as the officer motioned for Wilson to take Ed away.

"Sorry," Wilson muttered to the trooper as he nudged Ed down the steps and behind the yellow tape. "Keep out of the way until I can take you home, and don't cross the line again," he ordered Ed.

"I've got to get a complete story here, Chief," Ed countered. "It's my job."

"And my job is to keep unauthorized persons outside the tape, and that means you. Get all the story you can from that side." Wilson immediately started prowling the yellow tape strung around the perimeter of the area the state troopers considered the most germane to the night's events.

Ed wasted no time approaching every cop at the scene, but apparently they had a gag order and brushed him off. He approached the paramedics as they emerged with the wounded, but "Out of the way!" was the only response from them as they hurried their gurnied burdens to the ambulances. Ed tried to get a good look at the wounded, but the oxygen masks and med-paks on them prevented a decent identification. At least they weren't killed, Ed thought, as the ambulances hurried away. Finally, having been refused information by everyone there, he had to content himself with writing a narrative of the action at Miller's farm.

Ed was leaning on Wilson's cruiser watching the final stages of the police work when the chief and Pollard joined him.

"Pile in, Ed. I'll take you home now." Chief

Wilson was gray faced with the long night's chores and wasted no time entering his car and starting the engine.

"The Chief looks a little rough, doesn't he?" Ed said confidentially to Pollard, who walked beside him to the passenger side of the car.

Pollard briefly appraised Ed and replied, "You look pretty crappy yourself," and immediately moved on.

Pollard's curt remark suddenly made Ed aware his head was pounding like a bass drum, and as he got into the cruiser, he wondered why he hadn't felt it until now. Both cars were under way as he slammed his door.

Wilson glanced over at Ed. "When you write this up, Ed, make sure it's a little lurid. I want the nitwits out there who think they can take the law into their own hands to find out it can be a bloody business. That they're not playing kid's "Robin Hood" bullshit."

Ed, looking at Wilson's bloodshot, soot-circled eyes replied, "Folks will blanch with horror when I'm done, but don't plan on Mac letting it get printed that way. 'We're not a friggin' tabloid,' he likes to say."

"Whatever," Wilson responded tiredly.

The rest of the return ride to Portledge was in silence. Ed concentrated on his headache and had no idea what his chauffeur was thinking. As he watched the sun rise he decided to have Wilson drop him at the newspaper. He was afraid if he went home he'd sleep through the news deadline, Ted would get the Miller story from hearsay and hack out his usual watery version of what had happened. Wilson complied with Ed's request and explanation and dropped him at the Telegraph's door.

Ed entered the empty silence of the newsroom.

He grabbed Ted Jordan's electric typewriter from his fussily tidy desk, and sat at his own cluttered desk to write, thoroughly enjoying the use of a relatively modern piece of equipment. After an hour of write, ink eraser and rewrite, he left the article in Mac's office with a note explaining how he happened to be at Miller's farm, and that he was going home to snatch some sleep. He knew Mac would call him if there were any problems with the story.

It only took twenty minutes for Ed to walk home. The morning commuters and fellow walkers all stared at him with interest and he wondered why until he saw himself in a store window. His hair stood on end, his clothes were disheveled and glancing down at himself, he noted several rents in his teeshirt where the screwball had grabbed him. He was grateful to return to the refuge of his apartment.

Unfortunately, the terror of the night still hung in the air like Hollywood spider webs and Ed walked around the apartment double-checking the locks on the windows and doors. He saw where the man had entered. The bathroom window was jimmied and the old twist lock snapped in half. The bathroom, located on the other side of the apartment from his bedroom, accounted for his not hearing the noise. Ed slid the window shut and jammed the johnny brush between the lower window and the upper frame, hoping it would serve as a lock until the landlord could fix it. Still feeling insecure, he rummaged through the little tool chest he had stashed in a closet, dug out a ballpeen hammer and a small crowbar, and hefted both in his hands, pondering their possibilities. He dragged his overstuffed chair to the wall of the livingroom that faced all the accesses to the room, wrapped an Afghan over his shoulders and, weapons clutched to his chest, he fell asleep.

The late morning arrived like a dirty garbage truck, rumbling thunder and gray sheets of rain. Ed jerked awake. The hammer and crowbar clattered to the floor. A panicky look around reassured him he was alone. Painfully, he stretched his cramped limbs, rubbing the sore spots, and slowly stood up. He hobbled to the window, squinted out into a dreary downpour and wished he were in Florida, Hawaii or some other sunshine heaven, then suddenly remembered the "carte blanche" he got from Mac the night before, and his day brightened.

Ed wandered into the kitchen. It was its usual homey ambience. To make room to cook, he set most of the dirty dishes into the sink, filling it, so he shoved the rest of them to the rear of the counter. This morning's meal required him to scrape out the frying-pan to cook eggs and eat off a styrofoam plate with a plastic fork as he stood at the sink staring blankly out the window.

The phone rang as he mopped up the last of his egg with toast. He tucked the lightly greased receiver between his shoulder and ear.

"Yeah, Riley here," he mumbled through the toast.

"Eddie, it's Annie. Where have you been? I've been calling since seven."

"Hi, Annie. How're you?" Ed cheered even more. She had never called him before. "I was on a call with Wilson all night. Big doings at the Miller farm. I must not have heard the phone."

"I just got a call from some guy." She seemed not to care about Miller's farm.

"So? That should make you happy," replied Ed, suddenly deflated.

"It doesn't."

The last thing he wanted to be was her big brother, but it looked like it was headed that way. "What's the matter?" he asked, trying to adjust to the unwanted role.

"He threatened to kill me, that's what!"

"What!" His plate and fork dropped into the sink. " What did he say?"

"He said I'd better not shoot my mouth off to you no more, or I'd get the same thing Mark got."

The language sounded familiar.

"Everything was "dese" and "dose"," she added.

"He might be the same ape who broke into my apartment last night and smacked me with a pistol and double-negatives."

"You were attacked in your own place?" Annie's tone was sharp with fear.

"Listen, Ann, he's only trying to scare us off, especially me, being a reporter. I don't think you have to worry about it."

"You egotistical mutt," she snapped back. "I worked with Mark. If anybody has to worry, it's me, not some wet behind the ears reporter."

"All right, all right. You worry too. Meanwhile, I'll tell Wilson about this. He'll keep an eye out for you."

"No, don't do that," Annie hastily ordered.

"Why not?"

"He has enough to do. Besides, if there were any more cop cars hanging around Torrences', we'd lose the few clients we have left."

"Okay. I won't mention it, but you call me if anything more happens. I should be out there again today or tomorrow."

"I'll be watching for you, Eddie."

Chapter 6

Although Ed had counseled Annie to be unconcerned about her phone call, it alarmed him enough to get him out the door in a hurry. It was time to give his statement at the police station, anyway. While there, he hoped to find if there were any new developments with the Posse thing, not to mention his own. The jailhouse was just a short drive from his apartment, and parking was convenient.

"Hey, Riley. Move that crate of yours. It's in a no parking zone."

As Ed slammed his car door, he looked up to see Officer Pollard steaming toward him like the Queen Mary. He could envision a wake billowing up on either side of the man.

"Hello, Pollard. Get any sleep?"

"Move your heap, kid, or you'll find it in the pound."

"C'mon, Officer, I'm here on a story. The press should have a few perks, don't you think? Besides, Wilson's expecting me."

"I'll just bet he is. He ain't even in the office."

"Well, there's no law against waiting for him," responded Ed, as he edged past Pollard's bulk and walked through the door.

The front room was empty except for the dispatch officer, Willa Jean. She was in her phone booth-sized office filing her nails and barely glanced at him. Not much crime this morning, thought Ed.

Pollard hadn't followed him in, so with one eye on Willa, Ed casually strolled into Wilson's office and spent several minutes leafing through memos and reports on the desk. He was reading a report about confiscated automatic weapons and reputed war games on yet another abandoned farm in another part of the state when he was interrupted.

"Hello, Baby," a husky, breathy voice said.

Ed dumped the paperwork and spun to face the door. "Oh, Julie, it's you," he said, only partially relieved. Why was she here and where was Wilson?

"Oh, Julie, it's you," mocked the sheriff's daughter. "That's not a nice way to say hello." Her faced was clothed in its perennial pout.

Ed flashed a smile and asked, "What gets you up so early? It's barely sunrise." She looked smudged and rumpled, as though she hadn't gone to bed yet, or maybe it was too much bed.

Julie smiled sensuously as she neared Ed. "Haven't you ever wondered what it would be like to spend a little time with me, Eddie?" She tiptoed her fingers up Ed's arm, while pressing her centerfold breasts against his chest. Her pot-scented, bleached hair trailed over her shoulders, framing a heart-shaped face with bluer than blue eyes, thanks to tinted contact lenses, and a rosebud mouth.

Ed tensed, laughed weakly, and replied, "Well, hey, Julie, I'm a busy guy, you're a busy girl. Guess we never found time."

She formed her body against the length of him

and stroked down his back and buttocks with educated hands, pushing Ed's long unused buttons and momentarily canceling his headache. For an instant he forgot where he was and figured what the hell, everybody else has scored with her, why not him. He placed his hands in lovely places and his mouth against hers.

The office door slammed against the wall with a crash.

"Daddy!" Julie squealed and tore away from Ed's hard embrace.

"You son-of-a-bitch! What do you think you're doing with my daughter?" Wilson's teeth were bared in rage and the cords of his neck could have been strummed like a banjo.

Just what everyone else does, was on the tip of Ed's tongue, but a rare attack of good sense and a solid dose of fear made him say, "Well, I...she was here, and I..." Ed failed to hold Wilson's attention.

"Julia, get home—right now!" Wilson roared, momentarily ignoring Ed, "And don't you dare leave there until I talk to you!"

"Okay, Daddy," she said sweetly as she trailed out of the office. On her way by Ed, she stuck her tongue out at him.

Wilson swung back to Ed. "Where do you get off, kissing my daughter in my office?" His face, scant inches from Ed's, flamed scarlet as an August tomato and his fists formed hammers at his sides.

"I came in t-to give my statement," Ed stuttered, "and she came on to me."

"Bull! You took advantage of her. You bums are always after her."

This man suffers severe delusions about his little girl, thought Ed, but he knew better than to argue. "I'm sorry, Chief. It'll never happen again, I promise," and he cautiously moved toward the door.

Wilson grabbed him by the shirt and barked into his face, "I better never see you within fifty feet of her. Ever! Got it?"

The attack unnerved Ed. "Oh, yes, sir, never again, sir," he babbled as Wilson threw him out of the room and slammed the door shut.

Ed smoothed down his crushed shirt and looked up to see Pollard grinning at him from his desk.

"Enjoying yourself?" Ed asked him, sourly.

"Oh yeah," he chortled happily. "I'm delirious," and, laughing, he followed Ed out the door.

Ed could still hear him as he drove away, a parking ticket flapping under the wiperblade.

Ed knew he could safely count out Chief Wilson as a source of information. He had a feeling Julie had just paid him back for his stolen car report. She sure got her money's worth. Not only that, he hadn't given his required statement. That, too, would come back to haunt him.

While cruising aimlessly, he came to the conclusion that the farm held the answers to most of his questions. Maybe another trip there would shake them loose. Now, at least, he had a direction to drive in. A talk with Annie was in order. Maybe she could remember more of the phone call she'd received. Also, he wanted to check around for the murder weapon again. He hadn't seen any indication that it had been found during his hurried search through Wilson's papers. One thing he had noticed was a report noting that Joey Lorenzo had been brought in for questioning, then released. No alibi was mentioned. A forgotten

LEAD A DEAD HORSE TO WATER   53

memory suddenly struck Ed. He had seen Joey Lorenzo driving past him when he went to Torrences' the morning Mark had died. He wasn't going back to town to tell Wilson, though. An omission like that had to be reported, of course, but a cooling off period between him and Wilson made a lot of sense right now.

Although he hadn't heard from Mac, a visit to the office was probably in order just to make sure his farm raid story stayed intact. His entry into the newsroom was a balm to his Wilson-battered self-confidence.

"Hey, Eddie boy. Nice job on the Miller farm. Lucky break," said Marge, the society reporter.

"Way to go, Ed!" congratulated Willie, the Telegraph's lanky, good-natured janitor.

"Keep your damn hands off my typewriter," threatened Ted. Ed had forgotten to replace it on Ted's desk.

Ed just grinned at Ted and the rest on his way to Mac's office. He remembered to knock and wait for the invitation to enter.

At a wave of Mac's hand, Ed slung his slender frame into the hard oak chair in front of Mac's wide oak desk and smiled expectantly. He wasn't disappointed.

Mac beamed back. "Two major stories in two days! You're having an incredible run of journalistic luck, kiddo. How's your head?"

"Thanks, boss, and the head's fine," Ed lied. Actually, he was seeing spangles in front of his eyes occasionally and the pain from his goose egged scalp was throbbing. "Being with Wilson last night was a big break." He didn't mention it wasn't likely to happen again in the near future.

"There was a report about something similar over in Rutgers County a few months ago. Who'd think we'd have something like that happening around here?" Mac shook his head in disbelief. "People are getting wackier every day." He slapped the desk surface with his beefy palm.

Ed winced as the sharp thump echoed off his thumping head. "I'll do a follow up by tomorrow morning. The people I recognized will probably be out on bail and back in town by sometime today."

Mac held his hand up like a stop sign. "No, son, you keep after the Torrence story. I want Ted to mop up the farm raid. He's already agitating for it and I don't want to spread you too thin."

"Hey, wait a minute..." Ed protested.

"No arguments." Mac stood and leaned over his desk, burly arms propping his bulk. "Torrence is more important and that's the in-depth piece I want you on. Now, go. Get digging."

Ed stood abruptly, barely mollified by the Torrence assignment. Miller's was his, damn it. He had been there. But the hardened set of Mac's face allowed for no further negotiations. Resentful, Ed left the newspaper office faster than he had entered, trying, with considerable effort, to acknowledge the continued congratulations of his colleagues.

Chapter 7

As Ed drove to the Torrence farm, he decided to talk to Marlena before Annie. He parked in the lot just past the main house. Mark had been dead only one day, and physically, nothing had changed at the farm since then, but as Ed stepped out of his car, he could feel a heavy atmosphere that had cast a negative charge in the air, like a precursor to a thunderstorm about to break. While walking to the main house from the parking area he noticed that the usual morning bustle around the barn was gone. The few people he saw appeared grim and preoccupied. This was a far cry from the stable's normal cheerfulness. Ed knocked on Marlena's front door, expecting her usual banshee behavior.

"Marlena, hey, Marlena," he yelled through the door. She didn't answer. Ed pushed it open and stepped inside. It was gloomy and dank in the hallway with boots, whips and old coats in heaps in the corners, rather like entering the house through a cluttered closet.

The deadly quiet worried him. Marlena always had either the T.V. or the radio at ear-splitting decibels, even at eight-thirty in the morning. He crept down the hall into the kitchen, then through the dining room to the livingroom. No Marlena and no noise. Not at all normal.

Nerves on edge, Ed started up the stairs to the bedrooms. With each step he took, dirt gritted under his feet, the silence deepening as he reached the top. Cautiously, he slid around the corner.

There was an sharp explosion as the woodwork flew apart by his arm. He dropped to the floor and scuttled backward to the stairs. As he crouched on the top step, bugeyed, he heard a groggy voice.

"Who's there?"

"Marlena, is that you?" said Ed, hoarsely,

"Damn right. Who're you?"

"It's Ed Riley. Don't shoot!" It seemed guns had become awfully common lately, and it scared the hell out of him.

Pistol in hand, she weaved around the corner, peered down the steps and focused on him. "You look like a frog!" She laughed uproariously as she leaned against the wall. Her shapeless nightgown resembled her perennial robe; a food-spattered sampler.

Ed stood, gathered his tattered dignity and listened to her helpless convulsions while he glanced around. Some rooms were visible from where he stood. Every one had been trashed. The dressers had their drawers pulled out, the mattresses were on the floor, even the rugs were flipped back. It reminded him of the downstairs entry. Finally Marlena subsided, wiped her nose with the back of her hand and broke into tears.

"Eddie, what the hell is going on? Look what somebody did to my place," she wailed.

"When did it happen?" Ed asked, reaching up to stick his finger into the bullet hole in the woodwork at the level his elbow had been. A couple inches to the left and I'd be in bad shape. The thought made his heart clench.

"Last night," she replied and hiccuped.

"Last night?" Ed said in disbelief. What time?"

"I dunno. I came after him with my gun, and he ran outta here like a rabbit."

"Did you call the cops?" He winced as a splinter slid into his exploring digit.

"It was so scary, Eddie, I had to have a little nerve medicine to calm down. I guess it put me to sleep before I had a chance to phone them."

Nerve medicine. His father had called it nerve medicine too. Only, it put him to sleep for good. From the looks of Marlena, she was headed for a permanent nap herself.

"Anything happen before you went to bed last night that might indicate who it was?" Ed doubted she could remember much of the previous evening.

"I had a couple little drinks with Ben and he was asking me a bunch of dumb questions." She slid down the wall to sit next to Ed at the top of the steps. Her hand, draped over a raised knee, still held the gun.

"What kind of questions?"

"Don't know," she mumbled. "Business stuff and something about some legal papers Mark had. I forget. Get me the bottle from my nightstand, Eddie. My head is starting to hurt."

"No way, Marlena. We're going to have a little chat with Ben and see what he's been up to. Maybe he trashed your place."

She laughed harshly. "That jerk? He may a little snotty with his students, but he couldn't trash an empty bag. Mark's been carrying him for years."

"Why's that?"

"I guess now Mark's dead it doesn't matter anymore if I tell." She paused a moment. "Mark told me he and Ben were cellmates a long time ago. They got out at the same time and Mark couldn't get rid of him. Ben stuck like a leech even after Mark and I were married. Mark played the numbers and won enough to buy this place. I thought Ben had a share, but Mark said no even though Ben came along with us when we moved here."

It astounded Ed to learn that Mark had served time. "What was he in for?"

"Ahh, he ran a little numbers racket out west somewhere. No big deal. He didn't even make big bucks with it but he had to serve three years."

"No kidding. Where did they learn horseback riding good enough to give lessons?"

"Mark was raised around a racetrack and worked at a fancy riding stable as a kid. He taught Ben what he knew so he could at least earn his keep."

"Did you love Mark, Marlena?"

"I used to."

"But why the drinking?"

"It's those damned horses!" she shouted. "I hate them! He loved 'em, and he's ignored me ever since we got those hayburners. I used to get most of his attention, but then he bought this place and those four-legged bitches hogged the show. At least it would seem normal if he had another broad, but HORSES!" She banged her fist on the dirty carpet, raising a puff of dust. Ed stared at Marlena, half in pity, half disgusted. He remembered all the times his mother had put his father, who had drunk himself into a stupor, to bed. Now here he was, about to do the same thing; haul a drunk off to the sack, if she'd let him. Afterward, he'd check the rooms for evidence. He knew he had to call Chief Wilson, too. That was something to look forward to. One go 'round with him today had fulfilled his daily dose of humiliation.

"C'mon, Mar, how about some sack time? You look a little bushed." Ed pulled her up from the floor and draped her arm over his shoulder.

"Thank you, Eddie," she slurred. "I shoulda given you a tumble years ago when I looked a little better." They staggered into her bedroom. He eased her into her bed, dragging the covers over her, then gently removed the gun from her hand and placed it on the dresser.

"That's okay, Marlena," he said, grinning, remembering her former beauty. "If you'd done it years ago, you would have been arrested for corrupting the morals of a minor."

She was giggling when he shut the door.

Still in no hurry to call Wilson, and being careful not to touch anything, Ed slowly walked around the other bedrooms. Considering the general condition of the house, it was hard to tell what was moved and what wasn't. Dust was smeared and chairs were tipped over and dragged away from the walls. Only Marlena could tell what part of this chaos was normal. Over the years, she and Mark had collected more junk than ten people and it was scattered everywhere. He gave it up as futile within twenty minutes.

The call to the police was less than successful.

"What is it with you, Riley? Maybe if you stayed away from there that place would be a lot calmer," Wilson boomed over the phone. "I'll be right out."

The receiver crashed in Ed's ear; he immediately called Mac.

After being filled in, Mac repeated his old standby. "Get the facts straight, Riley, and have the story in by deadline."

Holy cow, thought Ed, you'd think I was causing all this stuff to happen to the Torrences.

While waiting for Wilson to arrive, he looked for Ben and found him at the outdoor arena supervising a group of student riders. Like ducks in a row, they were going this way and that, trying to coax their animals with proper dressage. Ed thought back on his years of dressage training. He had learned to control his mount with nearly invisible movements of his hands and legs and subtle shifts of his weight. It was a highly disciplined method of horse control, one both the animal and rider had to learn. In the end, both the mount and his master made horseback riding look effortless and elegant.

"Hello, Ben. How are you?" Ed asked.

Ben swung around to face Ed and replied, "I'm still living," and turned back to his students.

"I'd like to ask you a few questions about your conversation with Marlena last night and what happened afterward."

"What are you talking about?" he queried sharply.

"She had a break-in last night."

Ben stared at Ed for a moment as if in surprise. "I guess you think I did it?"

"You did want some papers from her. What were they about?"

"Do you have an inspector's badge or something? Those papers are none of your business and had nothing to do with Mark's death."

"If they have nothing to do with his death, why don't you want to tell me about it?"

"The whole damn world will know what's in them once they're found, and right now it's nobody's business but mine."

"Sounds like Marlena's business, too. She's hurting pretty badly and shouldn't be harassed over some petty interests you and Mark had."

"Don't worry about her," he sneered. "Her kind always land on their feet."

"She's not as bad as you make out, Ben, and she really loved Mark."

"Yeah, well, so what. That's no reason for being a drunken wildcat."

"Marlena aside, I'm trying to find out who killed our mutual friend, and anything I can learn might help."

Ben ignored Ed while he shouted instructions to his milling band. Ed watched the mob trot from one end of the arena to the other, the riders fiercely concentrating on every move of themselves and their animals. It saddened him to think Mark would never teach him or anyone else ever again, and said as much to Ben.

Something inside Ben seemed to collapse, and he looked at Ed. "You want to find Mark's killer? Find whoever brought the cocaine here on a regular basis and stashed it in the hayloft, and I'll bet my own life that you'll find him."

"Do you mean Mark was dealing dope?" For a moment, Ed thought he was going to be sick. Mark had been the closest thing to a dad he'd had since his own father had died, and though Ed knew the guy wasn't perfect, he never would have figured him for a drug pusher.

"I don't think so. Ever since I first knew him he was dead set against the stuff. Probably someone who rides here uses this place for a drop. When I took Mark to where the bag was hidden, it had been removed. He told me I was hallucinating."

Still suspicious, Ed asked, "How come you didn't see something sooner?"

"There was never anything to see. Whoever was doing it was mighty familiar with the place and knew when to make his moves."

Ed felt a stab of relief at Ben's doubt about Mark's involvement, then asked, "Did you tell the cops this?"

"Yeah, they were here again early last night but didn't find anything, and Marlena was no help. Dead drunk as usual. I had to give Wilson a list of our patrons for questioning. They're going to love that. I bet I lose what's left of my students." He shook his head and walked back to the group in the arena.

In the world of crime, it's often hard to tell who the bad guys are, but somehow Ed couldn't picture Mark as one of them. If he was dealing drugs, he was one heck of an actor. Ed had never suspected a thing, hopefully because there was nothing to suspect. Annie had worked closely with Mark, and in all her conversations with Ed she had never so much as hinted there might be a problem. Still, if Ben knew about narcotics on the place, why didn't she? Why didn't I, he wondered. I was there often enough to pick up on that kind of information. Then again, he reasoned, being a reporter probably kept people from telling him a lot of interesting things.

Wilson still hadn't arrived, and the cool, dark recess of the barn looked inviting. Ed ambled over and poked his head in the open door hoping to find a certain yummy lady.

"Annie, you in there?"

Horses snorted in reply as Ed sniffed and sneezed. Hay dust, again! He wandered into the friendly half-darkness and patted the noses of the curious horses that thrust their heads over the open dutch doors to check him out. Disappointed that he had no treats, some promptly retreated. Ed wandered the length of both aisles, ending up at the tackroom, and heard Annie's voice come from behind the closed door.

"You what?" She sounded angry. There was a pause. "Listen," she snapped, "You just be quiet. I'll see you tonight, same time, same place. You got it?"

Suddenly, the tackroom door swung open, slamming into Ed's nose.

He yelped sharply, and clapped his hands over his nose, the blood spurting between his fingers.

"Eddie!" gasped Annie.

"Holy cow, Annie, I think you broke my nose!" Ed kept his hands to his face, tasting blood as it oozed over his lips and chin. Crimson splotches tie-died his blue shirt.

"I'm sorry, I didn't know you were there." She reached over to check the damage.

Ed angrily pushed her hand away, but she persisted.

"Take it easy. I'm not going to hurt you."

"Hah!"

She carefully examined him, gently pressing the bloody cartilage centered on his face, and announced, "It's fine. Just a lot of blood. You'll live to sniff out plenty of stories."

"It sure doesn't feel fine." He stroked the sides of his nose with his handkerchief and wiped away the blood. "Who were you yelling at, anyway? My nose wants to know."

"No one you know, nosey. Just tonight's date giving me a hard time."

"Why would you date him if he makes you that mad?"

"Oh, Eddie, drop it," she replied.

Ed looked closely at her. Charcoal-like smudges darkened her eyes and her usual healthy blush had faded. "Hey, Annie, I'm sorry about Mark. I didn't like being right this time."

"Yeah, you picked a heck of a time to fall down on your reputation." She sighed and looked around. "I can't imagine what will happen to this place with Mark gone. I don't see Marlena taking his place in any capacity. How's the investigation going?"

"Wilson's going to be here soon. Marlena had a break-in last night and her place was torn apart."

"What! Poor Mar, what could she possibly have that's worth anything? Everything in that house should be in a dumpster."

"Who knows. I asked Ben if he knew anything about it, but he claims he doesn't."

Annie made a wry face. "I'll be he knows a lot more about what happens around here than he admits."

"You're right about that. He just told me that he recently found bags of cocaine hidden in the hayloft."

She grew very still and whispered, "Cocaine? My God, was Mark into cocaine?"

"If he wasn't, his killer was," Ed replied.

"Did Ben tell Mark what he'd found?"

"Yeah, but Mark claimed he didn't know anything. Ben told Wilson about it when he was questioned."

"No wonder he's been flea combing this place," she replied. "Funny, he never asked me about it."

"If there are any drugs here, he'll find them."

"I doubt it. Whoever left that other stash here would be a fool to keep it here now."

"You're probably right," Ed agreed. "Wilson must be here by now. I'm going down to the house. You coming?"

"Yeah. Most likely he'll want to talk to all of us again, and I especially want to watch him interview Marlena," Annie laughed wickedly.

Chapter 8

Wilson, with Pollard, was pulling into the driveway as Ed and Annie rounded the corner of the house. The Chief sprang athletically from the driver's side with athletic ease, while Pollard rolled out of the passenger seat, the car's springs groaning in protest.

Everyone arrived at the kitchen door at the same time.

"Good morning, Chief," Ed said politely. Annie echoed him.

Wilson looked right through Ed and replied, "Good morning, Annie."

Ed checked his reflection in the kitchen window to see if he was invisible. Nope, he definitely was visible. He tried again. "I spoke with Marlena this morning, Chief, and she doesn't know who..."

"Check around the outside of the house, Deputy Pollard," Wilson ordered. "I'll speak with Mrs. Torrence." He shouldered Ed aside and knocked on the door.

Ed could hear Pollard snickering as he cruised around the corner.

Wilson knocked on the door again, and they all waited silently for Marlena. After a few minutes, he rapped once more, this time harder. He stepped back and examined the upper story windows, hooked his thumbs into his gunbelt and softly slapped his fingers against the smooth black leather.

"What do you suppose is keeping her?" he wondered aloud.

Ed examined the cloud formations, the weeds by the door, his fingernails. He had no intention of telling Wilson about Marlena's current condition. Tit for tat, you twit, he thought.

Looking unhappy, Pollard sailed around the corner of the house and rejoined the group. His shoes and pant cuffs were soaked from the dew in the tall grass. Ed grinned broadly at him, enjoying the man's discomfort.

After several minutes of watching the Chief pounding on the door and yelling Marlena's name, Ed could hear him audibly grinding his teeth in rage. Finally, Wilson's reluctance plainly visible, he turned to Ed.

"Riley, you called this in. Did you talk to Mrs. Torrence?"

Ah, the invisible man had acquired wrappings of information. "Yeah, Chief. We had a long conversation before I called you."

Ed continued, "We chatted about the break-in and about Ben. We also covered the history of Mark's ownership of the farm."

"Did you touch any of the evidence?" Wilson asked dangerously.

"No, I know better," Ed replied evenly.

"You'd better know better. What about Ben and the farm history?"

Ed filled him on what Marlena had told him about the previous evening's events.

"Hmm..." Wilson mused, his fingertips drumming his gunbelt as he stared at the ground. "Pollard, bang on that door. Get that woman's attention."

As Pollard thundered on the door, a second floor window above him flew open. Marlena thrust herself halfway out. "What the hell do you want? Can't a person get any rest around here?"

Startled, Pollard stumbled back from the door. The Chief looked up at her with a stony face, while Annie and Ed glanced at each other with barely suppressed grins. Wilson was going to have his hands full.

"Why, Chief Wilson," Marlena simpered drunkenly. "How nice of you visit the bereaved again. Do come in."

"Mrs. Torrence," Wilson replied sternly, "put a robe on and come downstairs, please."

Apparently she had been preparing for him, for she had changed into a see-through baby doll nighty. Ed noticed Pollard was gasping like a beached fish. She may have gained a few pounds, but a lot of them were in the right places. After a few moments, she flung open the kitchen door, waved her arm in a grand gesture and curtsied.

"Entré. So nice of you to call on me." She had put on make-up, but it wandered off her lips and eyes in smudges, her cheeks glowed a bright rose and her hair was teased and tangled into a Kansas twister. With a filmy wrapper loosely tied at her waist, she looked like a flower gone berserk.

Wilson's eyes narrowed and flickered over her. "Good morning, Mrs. Torrence," he greeted tonelessly. "Your call said you had an intruder last night. Can we go inside and talk about it?"

"Please do. It's been such a trial, being alone like this. It seems like everything is falling apart around me." Bumping into the doorjamb, she swung around in a grand manner and swept into the house.

The group, while still assimilating the sight of Marlena, gingerly stepped through the door into the kitchen. The counters and table were covered with food-crusted crockery, lipstick-ringed glasses, and ashtrays flowing over with cigarette butts.

"Have a seat, everyone. There're enough chairs, I think." Marlena pushed the clutter on the table to the center and wiped the crumbs to the floor with unsteady hands. Everyone but Wilson and Pollard sat down.

Not a muscle twitched in Chief Wilson's face as he watched her. "Is there anything you can tell us about last night? Did you recognize the intruder?" he questioned.

"I heard him but was too scared to leave the bedroom. Then I remembered Mark's revolver in the bedtable drawer and started screaming I'd shoot. I must have scared him off."

"Too bad you didn't scream at me," Ed said with a wry smile.

"What's that supposed to mean?" growled Wilson.

"What it means," said Marlena, "is that I took a potshot at Eddie when he came up the steps this morning. Lucky for him I missed."

"Too bad," Pollard whispered loudly.

Wilson shot his deputy a pointed look, then asked the two women and Ed to stay downstairs. With Pollard lumbering along behind, Wilson spent several minutes examining the upstairs portion of the house. Still seated at the table, the trio could overhear snatches of the policemens' conversation. The words "mess" and "sty" floated down the steps, but even better was the name "Lorenzo," which caused the little group to lean in unison toward the stairs.

The officers must have thought no one could

hear them, for they could hear Wilson tell Pollard he would talk to Lorenzo again that evening, and maybe Joey's drug history and the cocaine found on the farm were tied in together. Their voices trailed away as they worked their way down the hallway. Later, they thudded down the steps and examined the rooms on the first floor.

Finally, Wilson approached Marlena. "Mrs. Torrence, I'm going to request the county crime investigation unit come out here this afternoon to take some fingerprints, so please don't clean upstairs until he does." He and Pollard walked to the door. "Don't worry," he assured. "We'll find the culprit before too long and have him behind bars." Then he and Pollard quickly left.

Ed had the feeling the cops were escaping rather than leaving.

"Well, how do you like that? You'd think he'd stay longer what with all the terrible things happening here," complained Marlena while she rubbed her face, smearing the clown-like makeup into a colorwheel on her face.

Annie, familiar with the house's disorder, rummaged through the cupboards for a clean glass. "Don't let it bother you, Marlena. I'm sure he has all the information he needs from here but has to question lots of folks." She gave up on finding anything clean in the cupboard, and washed one that was sitting in the sink among the other dirty dishes.

Ed thought it might be the reek of decaying food in the garbage can and the leftover caked dishes that had sent Wilson out the door so fast. He glanced at his watch. "Oh man! I'd better get going. My deadline is coming fast. See you gals later."

"Hey, Eddie, what's gonna be in this story?"

Marlena asked seriously. Her drunkenness seemed less pronounced.

Ed realized she was worried that he'd make a fool of her in print. Reassuring her, he said, "Only the break-in, Marlena. I want to cover this story in depth, but I'm not out to hurt you."

As he left, she was still sitting at the table, pensively tracing a pattern on the table with her fingertip. Annie flipped him a wave with a sudsy hand.

Chapter 9

It didn't take Ed long to write up the Torrence business. All the juicy stuff was off the record. Mac read it over.

"Kind of dry, Riley. What happened to your usual exhibitionism?"

"Wasn't much to see, boss. The whole house was screwed up and Mrs. Torrence wasn't feeling well."

"You mean drunk."

"I figure she has enough problems without us smearing her all over the front page."

"Yeah, let it go. What else do you have?"

"I'm going to hunt up Joey Lorenzo. Wilson thinks there's a connection between him and the cocaine found at the farm."

"And just how do you happen to know that piece of information? Never mind, I don't want to know." Mac nervously rubbed his seamed face with beefy hands that looked out of place on a desk jockey. "Oh, man. Watch yourself while you're out there, kid. Some of the places he might frequent could be rough as hell," he admonished, then retreated to his office. Mac watched with worried eyes as Ed left the office.

Ed arrived at the address he'd found in Joey's file on Chief Wilson's desk and knocked at the door, but no one answered. Luckily, the apartment was on the ground floor, allowing him to peek through the windows and the kitchen door on the back porch. Joey's decor was the same as his own, dirty dishes and disarray. He was startled by a raspy voice.

"What the hell do you think you're doing there?" An old guy with wispy, white hair and a shabby teeshirt leaned over the fence of the adjacent yard and stared suspiciously at Ed.

Instantly, Ed altered his personality, becoming the young man everyone likes, and walked over to join him. "Good afternoon, sir. Have you seen Mr. Lorenzo recently?"

"Mr. Lorenzo," the old man snorted. "Who wants to know?"

"He and I are old friends, and I dropped by for a visit."

"You look too respectable to be a friend a' his. In fact, you kinda look like a baby cop."

Ed laughed genially, "No, sir, not a cop, but if you'll tell me where I might find Joseph, I'd appreciate it." He reached into his pocket, and held out a five dollar bill.

Snatching the money from Ed's hand, the old man stared hard at it, spat to one side, and said, "Is this the best you can do?" After a quick glance at Ed's beet-colored face, he continued. "Try Billy's Bar later tonight. I hear he goes there sometimes." He stuffed the bill into his pocket and retreated to his house of peeling paint.

Ed walked away, doubting the old guy. He didn't think his lame "respectful youth" act or the money got him that pittance of information; then again, maybe Joey pulled a fast one on the oldtimer, and he was getting even.

Ed killed time in the local diner having supper and kidding around with the new waitress, Janine, a replacement for Emily, who was arrested at the Miller farm raid.

"Yeah, Em's gone. They hired me this morning," Janine said as she plunked down a cup of coffee in front of Ed.

"You'd think they would have held her job for her, at least for a while...not to say you shouldn't be here," Ed added hastily.

"Customers won't wait on themselves, Eddie. Besides," Janine added confidentially, "I hear Emily was snorting something and talking a lot of racial garbage recently. She even talked about arresting the federal judge that has session here in town. Seems that group she belongs to has it in for him. Guess he's safe for a while, after last night."

"How could they arrest a judge?" Ed had heard of citizen's arrest, but busting a judge was a little far-fetched.

"Beats me. Emily said they could arrest anyone they thought was breaking the law, but they had to take their prisoner straight to the county sheriff." She shrugged her shoulders and returned to the counter with Ed's supper order.

What kind of organization lunatic was that, Ed wondered, as he worked his way through an open steak sandwich, coleslaw and French fries. Arresting judges, weapons caches (If that event involved the same group), drug deals. Wilson mentioned the "Posse". Maybe a little visit to the library was in order.

The brightening streetlamps silently announced the end of daylight. I should have gone home, Ed thought, while sipping his third and last cup of coffee, but the sink full of crusted dishes and laundry all over the floor makes me feel as though I'm at Torrences'. Goodbye, appetite.

Billy's Bar was long, dark and narrow. It reeked of smoke and stale beer. The bar ran along the left side of the room, and tables, with their attendant mongrel chairs, to the right. The plate glass door reflected the streetlight inside as Ed entered.

Several people turned and stared suspiciously as he glanced around for Joey then walked the length of the room. Ed spotted Lorenzo at the end of the bar hunched over a beer and joined him.

"Joey, how you doing?" Ed asked cheerfully.

"Screw off," Joey muttered.

Ed ignored the rude dismissal, edged onto the next stool and leaned toward Joey, confidentially. "Saw your file on Wilson's desk, Joey. Don't worry. He doesn't have anything on you."

Joey nervously licked his lips and glanced at Ed. "I dunno what you're talking about."

"I also heard him tell Pollard to check you out because of an attempted burglary at Torrences', and how about that act of terrorism in my apartment last night? You know that I know it was you, but who was your pal at the farm?"

"I don't know nuthing about nuthing at no farm, and it sure as hell wasn't me in your place," he hissed, then sucked on his beer.

"Voices don't lie, Joey. The illiterate hassling me last night is the same one sitting here right now."

"Yeah? You musta been talking to yourself!"

Ed continued over Joey's limp joke. "And I distinctly remember seeing your car passing mine on my way to Mark's the morning he died. What were you doing out that way so early? Who's your partner, Joey? Is he the one who killed Mark? Did he scare Marlena last night?"

The bartender ambled down and rested his football-sized hands on the edge of the bar. "You want a drink, Bub?"

"No thanks, I..."

"Sure you do." He grabbed Ed's arm and winked at Joey. "What'll it be, Sonny, near beer or a Pink Lady?"

Joey sauntered out of the bar while Ed kept one eye on the menacing bartender and choked down the Pink Lady.

Ed glanced at his clock again. Eight a.m. The static of the police scanner crackled annoyingly as he burrowed under his pillow trying to ignore it. The same old stuff had been coming over the airwaves for the last half hour: dogs taking a crap in the neighbor's yard, a kid on a school bus showing an 8 X 10 glossy pornographic photo to the drivers following behind him. Ed wondered if the kid's Mommy knew Daddy had those pics, or was it vice-versa? All the news too stupid to print floated into the room.

Ed had drifted back into a light doze when the number "187" crackled from the scanner into the room. Murder! "187" meant a murder. Ed catapulted from bed, flung on his clothes, and bolted out the door. He barreled through traffic with his press sign in the window, while groping around the front seat for some scattered mints to allay the crummy taste in his mouth. The address Ed had jotted down was familiar, very familiar.

"Oh God," he groaned softly as he arrived at Joey Lorenzo's house.

All the Portledge police cars, three, lined the front of the house. The local housewives, many in bathrobes, crowded the sidewalk with cups of coffee in hand. Ed pinned his press identity card to his shirt and elbowed his way through. Longmeyer stopped his progress at the door.

"No admittance, kid," he said with nasal superiority, adopting a body-blocking stance. His skinny frame resembled an anorexic scarecrow.

"One, I'm not a kid, Longmeyer, and two, I have a press pass." Ed flipped his identity card on his chest with one finger as he attempted to pass.

"Wanna bet?" Longmeyer grabbed Ed by the shoulder. "Wilson says no admittance to anyone until he and the county crime unit investigates the scene. He specifically mentioned you."

Ed angrily shrugged off the deputy's hand. "At least tell him I'm here. I've got some information about Joey he might be interested in." Ed strained around Longmeyer to see into the house. "I guess Joey's dead, huh?"

"What makes you think Lorenzo's dead?"

"Oh, come on, Longmeyer, I know this is Joey's place and what the number "187" means when it comes over the scanner."

"Okay, kid, hang around, kid, I'll tell Wilson you're here when he comes out." Longmeyer rested one hand on his bullet studded gunbelt, the other he wrapped around the pistol handle, as though he would yank it from its holster should Ed try to get by him again.

Ed's eyes traveled from the warning position of Longmeyer's hand to the scowl on his face, and decided not to push it. He'd get to see what had happened to Joey soon enough. He smiled insolently at the bristling deputy, and went back down the steps.

Well, thought Ed, since he couldn't get into the house right away, maybe the guy next door could shed some light on the subject. He had been happy enough to clue him in on Billy's Bar once he'd been greased. Ed checked his pockets for another fiver on the way over.

The object of Ed's redirected attention was on his front porch slouched on a broken chaise longue. He wore faded, bagged out slacks held up by suspenders, and a frayed teeshirt under a torn flannel shirt worn against the morning chill.

As Ed approached the steps he announced to the porch occupant, "Good morning. I'm Ed Riley, the reporter from the Telegraph. They shook hands.

"Why, good mornin', son. I'm Charlie Smith. Nice to see you again." Then he cackled a laugh. "I knew you was trying to pull a fast one on me yesterday. I knew you wasn't no friend of Lorenzo's. So you're the one been writing about the killing. Real interesting readin'."

"Thanks, Charlie, I appreciate that." Ed placed his right foot on the first step, and leaned forward in a confidential manner. "Say, can you tell me anything about what's happened next door?"

Charlie chuckled at Ed. "I heard a hell of a fight at Lorenzo's last night, so I decided to keep an eye on the place. I like to keep up with the neighborhood doin's."

I'll just bet you do, thought Ed as he whipped out his notebook and pen from his jacket pocket. "What time did you hear the fight?"

"Let's see," replied Charlie. Thoughtfully, he rubbed his stubbly jaw. "It was about four a.m. I was standing at the kitchen window, kinda gazing out at nothin', when I heard stuff smashing and some yelling, mostly Lorenzo, I think. It went on for fifteen or twenty minutes. It was a big brawl even for this neighborhood. Then it got real quiet. The lights went out and I seen some little guy sneaking out the back door."

"Didn't he notice you at the window?"

"Naw. I didn't have my light on. I'm up a lot in the night what with an old man's aches and pains. Got so's I get along just fine in the dark. Besides, there's always interesting doings on this street after that old sun goes down. If my light was on, I wouldn't get to see any of it," he replied, and lit a cigarette.

"You say it was a small man who left?" Ed asked as he scribbled furiously in his notebook.

"Yeah, quick, too. He was gone before I could get to the door to see which way he went."

"Was it you who called the police?"

Charlie squinted at Ed through bloodshot eyes, and sucked his lips over tooth-sparse gums. "This is strictly off the record. You never heard me say this. I did call about seven-thirty this morning, but I'll never admit it around witnesses, so don't you be sticking my name in your paper. I meant to call earlier, but I sat down in my easy chair to think on it and fell plumb asleep."

"Night life is tough," Ed agreed with a grin. "How come you don't want the cops to know you called?"

"Ah, cops is a pain. They wanta know everything about you soon as you open your mouth to 'em."

"Don't you worry, Charlie. I'll never tell them you called."

"That's a good boy." Charlie wheezed as he lit a cigarette off the previous one, the third since Ed had joined him on the porch.

"Riley, hey, Riley! Get over here," Longmeyer yelled from Lorenzo's front stoop.

"Be right there," Ed shouted. He turned again to Charlie. "Thanks for everything. I'd like to come back later for some information on Joey if you don't mind."

"Sure, sonny. Just remember, as far as the cops are concerned, I don't know nuthin'."

Ed smiled and winked at him. "You bet. Catch you later."

Chapter 10

Ed returned to Lorenzo's house. On the way he heard a falsetto voice from the ranks of the housewives, "Riley, oh Riley. Get over here!"

Longmeyer leered at him, "Got a friend out there, honey?"

Ed ignored the remark.

Longmeyer continued, "What was that old bum telling you?"

"He told me he didn't know nuthin'," Ed snapped, and brushed past the deputy to find Chief Wilson.

People from the county crime investigative unit were packing their equipment and the evidence they had gathered. Ed met Wilson in the front room. The previous day's uproar still fresh in Ed's mind, he waited for the Chief to speak first.

Apparently, Wilson hadn't forgotten Ed and Julie's clinch either, for his tone was decidedly unfriendly.

"So...Riley. I didn't think I'd get through this morning without you. In fact, I'm surprised you didn't call this in."

Ed ignored Wilson's sarcasm and asked, "Where's Lorenzo?"

"In the kitchen," Wilson replied curtly. "Take a look around. See if you recognize anything."

Joey's livingroom was scrambled. Furniture had been toppled, lamps smashed and a large wall mirror lay in shards on the rug. The kitchen wasn't much better. The table was shoved against the wall, its chairs tipped over, and splintered glasses and plates were scattered across the floor from the dish drainer that had been knocked off the counter.

The worst sight, though, was Joey. He was slumped to one side in the corner by the back door. His head was cocked back to the right, and his throat was slashed. The same silver-handled knife Ed had seen in Mark was now hilt-deep in Joey's neck. Blood was splattered over cabinets, walls and floors, as though painted by a crazed impressionist. The sight of Mark in the stall was bad, but this was worse, much worse.

"Oh my God," Ed mumbled. He gagged and bolted for the door. Now he was glad there hadn't been time for breakfast.

"Pretty rank, huh Riley?" said Wilson, who had followed him outside. "You seem to be tied up with most of this case's disasters. What do you know about this one?"

"The knife," Ed replied as he rubbed his face with shaking hands. "It looks like the one used on Mark." He kept gulping back the nonexistent breakfast.

"That's what I thought you'd say. There's a drawer in the kitchen that has seven more just like it. Mighty nasty steak knives, I'd say." Wilson re-entered the house, leaving Ed to his dry heaves.

There now was no doubt in Ed's mind that Mark's and Joey's murders were done by the same person, but he was positive Wilson didn't care what he thought. Wilson would come to his own conclusions. As Ed waited for his heaving guts to subside, he mulled over what he knew.

Ben had found drugs at the farm, told Mark and bam!, Mark was killed. Now Joey's throat was cut, apparently with the same knife, and he had been at or near the farm the same morning of Mark's death. As for Ben, he could be lying. It was possible for him to be the murderer, and maybe Marlena had told one hell of a story, too. She and Ben had known each other a long time. Could be they were partners. Of course, there was Annie, but he doubted she had anything to do with all of this. Probably her biggest drug experience had been smoking a joint next to an open bedroom window when she was sixteen.

Maybe an old jailbird friend of Mark's was dealing dope with Joey, decided Joey had become a liability and killed him. Ed did not want to think Mark was a drug dealer.

Ed heard the coroner pronounce Joey dead and he watched as the paramedics bundled Joey's bagged body onto a gurney for the trip to the ambulance and ultimately, the morgue.

Reluctantly, Ed decided he had better tell Wilson about sighting Lorenzo and the thought added acid to his roiling innards.

Wilson rejoined Ed on the back porch and asked, "Can you think of anything else that would pertain to this case?"

Ed wondered if the man had been reading his mind. "I'm glad you asked that," he lied. "There are a few more things I should tell you."

"Here we go," Wilson said sourly. "What is it?"

Ed took a deep breath, braced himself and quickly said, "As I was driving to the farm the morning Mark died, I saw Joey's car pass me heading for town," and with a fresh squirt of stomach acid, he added, "and I saw Ben leave the barn at the time I entered that same morning, but for the life of me I don't know why I didn't remember any of this until just now."

Wilson shouted. "I should have you charged with obstruction of justice. What else have you got tucked away in that pea-brain of yours?"

"Nothing, Chief, honest!" Ed crossed his fingers behind his back. He wasn't going to betray Charlie.

Wilson stormed back into the house and Ed heard him tell Longmeyer to go out to Torrences' farm and arrest Ben Gordon on suspicion of murder, and don't forget to read him his rights. On second thought, Wilson reconsidered aloud, he'd better do it himself.

Wilson left Pollard behind to wrap things up in the house while he and Longmeyer headed for their cars.

Ed left with them. He hoped to arrive at the farm first, and although his vehicle was further away, he, unlike the cops, didn't have to creep through the curious crowd. Gloating at his luck, Ed drove away first. Miraculously, his clunker outdid itself and made an excellent getaway. He was about a mile ahead of the police when his gas gauge lived up to its liar's reputation. A few chokes and a dying gasp of the engine left him stranded by the side of the road. There were three more miles to Torrences' and Ed was now on foot.

"Damn, damn!" Ed yelled. He struck his fist repeatedly on the indifferent steering wheel. A small hope pricked him. Maybe Wilson would pick him up. He scrambled out of his car and stood at the side of the road, thumb out.

Moments later Wilson sped by, cruiser lights flashing. He didn't give Ed a single glance. The second police car, with Longmeyer at the wheel, approached him at a good clip, but slowed to a crawl as it neared him. Ed stuck his thumb out and grinned.

"Whatsa matter, Riley, outta gas?" Longmeyer yelled.

"How'd you guess?" Ed said, and laughed as he reached for the door handle.

Before Ed could touch it, Longmeyer peeled away, tires pelting gravel in a high arc. "It's against the law to hitchhike, Riley," yelled Longmeyer out the car window. "I better not catch you doing it again."

Cursing, Ed slapped the dirt off his clothes as Longmeyer's car flashed its way around the bend.

Chapter 11

Ed hoped to be at the farm when they arrested Ben, but he would have had to run like an Olympic champion to make it. A mini convoy, Wilson and Longmeyer, passed him at a good clip twenty minutes later. Ben was in the back seat of Wilson's car. Ed noted that Ben's face wore a stony frown. Longmeyer brought up the rear, grinning wolfishly at Ed, who was trotting down the road in the opposite direction. Ed doggedly slogged on, trying to ignore the shooting pains running up his legs and the strong side-ache clamped against his ribs.

I swear, Ed thought as he puffed down the road, I'm going on an exercise program. I'm too damn young to be this screwed up on a three-mile jog. Several minutes later he staggered up the farm driveway, running rivers of sweat and desperate for water.

For a moment he leaned against the house by the shaded kitchen door gasping for breath. The conversation inside grabbed his attention and he forced himself to breath quietly. He could hear Annie speaking over the sobs of Marlena.

"This is unbelievable! There's no way on earth Ben is a killer." Her tone was emphatic and certain.

Marlena wailed, "We knew and trusted him. Why would he murder Mark and Joey?"

"He didn't, but Wilson will think you know more than you're telling, Marlena. You've known Mark and Ben longer than anyone else in town, and I'm sure he'll be back soon, full of questions."

"Wonderful," muttered Marlena. "More crap from him. I'm tired of him and everything else around here. I want another drink."

"Marlena," Annie said firmly, "You have to help me now. Without Ben, I'm all alone in that barn, and even though I've tried to assure them that they're in no danger, every one of our student workers has left."

"Let me alone," snapped Marlena. "I have to take care of Mark's funeral and think about Wilson. I can't be bothered with horses." The sound of a bottle clinking on a glass followed.

"Damn you!" Annie yelled furiously. "Those horses are yours now, and they have to eat. The stalls have to be cleaned and what few student riders we still have need to be taught. I'll be damned if I'll do it all!" The smash of glass punctuated the sentence.

Ed quickly knocked on the door and stepped inside. The women were gripping the table, staring each other down. Pieces from the tumbler and whiskey bottle were strewn across the floor in pungent puddles of booze. It seemed to be a day for broken glass.

"Time out," Ed said as he made the football signal with his hands. "Let's just settle down, girls."

They both turned and glared at him, bonding in an instant.

"I don't see any girls in here, do you Marlena?" Annie spat.

"No. All I see is a hot, sweaty kid with shit for brains," Marlena replied, nastily.

"Okay, okay," Ed hastily amended. "I made a mistake; I didn't mean it. I apologize, okay? You're women, not girls, alright?"

They glanced at each other and shrugged simultaneously as if to dismiss his stupidity.

Ed quickly walked over to the sink for a glass of water. "Tell me what happened when Wilson and Longmeyer came for Ben."

"Not much to tell," replied Annie. "Ben was here, discussing the sad mess we're in, when Wilson knocked at the door. Ben answered and within five minutes he was gone. Kaput. Now there's only me to keep this place running unless Marlena gets off her dead rearend and helps me." She turned to Marlena. "This is your place, you know."

Marlena sighed and put her face in her hands. "I suppose it is. I never thought about that. Now what do I do?"

"You help me keep things going, that's what you do," Annie stated flatly. She looked at Ed. "What the heck are you doing?"

He was trying to scour out grease from the cleanest-looking cup in the sink. "I'm trying to get a drink after my morning jog."

"Yeah, right," she laughed. "You only jog when there's a horse under you."

"Not always. Sometimes I jog when heartless cops won't pick me up. I ran out of gas three miles from here."

Marlena leaned back in her chair and said to Annie, "Why don't you fill a gas can from the farm's gasoline tank and give him a ride back to his car?" She then turned to Ed. "No offense, Eddie, but I don't feel like talking to you today. Find some other story for tonight's headlines." She left the room crunching in scruffy slippers through the sharp litter on the floor. Still thirsty, Ed reluctantly set the greasy cup on the counter and followed Annie to find the gas can.

"Do you think she'll pitch in and help?" Ed asked. They had reached a small shed used to hold all the small items that defied storage elsewhere. Sort of like a giant kitchen flotsam and jetsam drawer.

"Who knows? She's been a pain ever since I came here, and I don't see how she could change overnight. I need help right now." Annie rummaged through the cluttered shed for a container. "Here's one," and she yanked a five gallon can from under a musty, rotted tarpaulin. They walked over to the large, above ground gasoline tank.

"Do you think Ben killed Mark and Joey?" Even though Ed had heard her defend Ben in Marlena's kitchen, he wanted to make sure she wasn't just trying to make Mar feel better.

"Heck, no! Ben Gordon wouldn't swat a horse-fly," she said as she pumped gas into the can.

"That's a good one. I thought he was going to kill the guy who punched that bay mare, Rita, in the nose for bucking him off." And that wasn't the only time he'd seen Ben irate regarding a student's treatment of a horse. Ed leaned against the upwind side of the cool storage tank. The odor on the other side was making him sickish.

"Well, of course," Annie replied. "Ben never allows anyone to mistreat the horses, but I have to admit he carries it a little far sometimes. As for murdering Mark or Joey, Ben doesn't even believe in corporal punishment, so there's no possibility he's their killer."

"Guess you know Ben pretty well, then?" Ed didn't want to acknowledge a sinking sensation regarding his hopes for Annie.

"Holy cow, Ed. He and I worked together every

day. We had conversations like all co-workers." She deftly twisted the cap back onto the gas can. "Well, Eddie," she said briskly as she handed him the can, "I've got to go now. Lots to do. Good luck with your car." She started walking quickly toward the barn.

"Hey, aren't you going to drive me there? This lousy can is heavy."

"Can't do it, Ed. Here comes my student now. See you later."

"Thanks a lot, Annie! I'll return the favor some day," he shouted at her rapidly retreating back. Ed looked down at the reeking, rusted container and hoped the damn thing wouldn't burst apart before he reached his car. Resolutely, he squared his shoulders, picked up the dead weight of the full five gallon container and trudged down the driveway. As Ed came abreast of the kitchen door, Marlena came out of the house dressed in jeans, boots and an old sweatshirt.

"Where are you headed in that getup, Mar?" He had rarely seen her in anything but bedclothes.

She glanced at Ed and tersely replied, "I'm going to clean a stall." She looked pasty without her usual mask-like makeup.

Ed set the already arm-stretching can down and stared in amazement at her back as she made her slightly unsteady way up the drive. I must be hallucinating from these gas fumes, he thought, as he watched her uncertain progress.

The business of getting the gas can filled had temporarily driven thirst from his mind, but now it became uppermost. He rattled the latch of the kitchen door and found that Marlena had locked it. Cursing aloud, he glanced up the drive to call her back, but she had disappeared into the cool gloom of the barn. With more muttered curses, he hefted the leaden weight of the gas can, and, shifting it from hand to hand as each shoulder, in turn, ached with pain, he walked the long distance back to his car.

Ed scuffed painfully into the newspaper office, two hours later, sweat soaked and dirty.

"What happened to you?" Madge asked. Her face revealed concern.

Ed related the morning's events, cursing Wilson and Longmeyer in the process. He privately cursed Annie, too, for inflicting the "Bataan Death March" on him.

She clucked her tongue in commiseration. "Well, I would certainly give them a piece of my mind if I were you, Eddie."

"Sure, Madge. I'll do that. Wilson would tear my head off."

At that moment, the senior reporter, Ted Russell, strolled through the door. As always, he was wearing a crisp white shirt, sedately patterned tie, plain buttoned vest and sharply creased slacks. He was immaculate right down to his shiny wingtips.

"How's the Torrence investigation coming along, Junior?" he asked, a secretive smile twisted onto his pale, gaunt face.

"It's doing fine, Ted, just fine," replied Ed, tiredly.

"That's good, Junior. You keep plugging away on it while I cover not only the Posse story; I'll take care of the Lorenzo piece, too." He fiendishly grinned at Ed and walked to his desk.

Exhaustion forgotten, Ed yelled, "What do you mean, you're covering Lorenzo? It's all part of the same story!"

"Two separate murders, two separate stories, Junior. You should be on your knees, grateful to have the Torrence line at all. By rights the whole thing should have gone to me," he bitterly replied. Ted turned to his electric typewriter and slid in a fresh piece of paper. At the end of each line of type, he smashed the return button as though wishing it were Ed's face.

Banging aside chairs and trash cans, Ed charged across the room to Mac's office. "We'll just see what the hell is going on here," he shouted back at Ted.

Ed furiously knocked on Mac's door and barged in barely before Mac waved him in.

Wearily, Mac looked up at him. "What's the matter, Riley, as if I didn't know."

Ed flung himself into the chair in front of Mac's desk. "What's the deal with Ted?" he demanded angrily. "You told me the Torrence case was my story. Now Russell has it and my Posse piece, too."

"Look, Ed, this is a big story. There are two deaths now, and I want both of you working on them. You're still just a junior reporter on this paper and you can't expect me to cut Ted out of the action completely, especially with Lorenzo killed. Besides, double coverage beefs up the paper's circulation." Mac leaned back, folded his hands across his broad stomach and beetled his brows at Ed.

Ed sprang up and leaned over the desk, scattering Mac's papers. "I was on the scene, not Ted. I identified the knife, not Ted. I want the story!"

"Is that so?" Mac's face turned red in anger. He stood abruptly, planted his fists on his disheveled desk and placed his face within inches of Ed's. "And I want you to sit down with Ted and give him a great interview with lots of color. The readers will love it." Mac pointed sharply to the door and ordered, "Go talk to him, and I don't want to hear any more bitching from you about who gets what assignment!"

Furious, Ed bolted from Mac's office to sit for several minutes at his desk, fuming. Wisely, everyone in the room left him alone, even Ted. As career reporters, they had all known the disappointment of losing plum assignments. After thirty minutes, Ed's volcanic eruption had simmered to a dull sheen on still hot magma and he resentfully gave Russell the interview, lathering it with psychedelic color. Later, when he thought about it, Ed realized that Ted had been a complete professional during the interview. He hadn't even called him junior. Be damned if he'd thank him, though.

Ed wrote his piddling little piece, too. Both stories landed on the front page. Ted got the headline, and Ed found his follow up story about Mark Torrence at the bottom of the page, next to the index. Maybe Pollard was right. Pretty soon poor Mark would be buried on the back page, and then forgotten completely. Ed got a bad feeling his rising star was suffering re-entry burn.

Chapter 12

The headlines were out and from the placement of his story, Ed thought glumly, it looked like he was out, too. Like his pre-Torrence pieces, it was slashed to a minuscule portion of what he had originally turned in.

Ed tossed his paper down in disgust. I don't know why I ever wanted to be a newspaperman in the first place, he groused silently. Ensconced in his apartment and licking his literary wounds, Ed spent the latter part of the afternoon slouched in his favorite ratty easychair flipping through the television channels and occasoinally kicking the mushroom-shaped hassock.

Increasingly cranky stomach rumbles reminded him food had been forgotten in the day's aggravations. He browsed the interiors of his cupboards and refrigerator, but found a famine, and decided to see what his mother had cooked for her dinner. She often cooked for several in the off chance family or friends might drop in, not an infrequent occurence. Tonight she'd have the pleasure of his company.

Ed drove his car into her driveway and found her on a ladder soaping down the kitchen windows of her one-story house.

"Crap," he moaned. "This probably means supper is out. She doesn't stop for anything when she gets into her cleaning mode."

Mrs. Riley was a housecleaning fanatic. Every nail hole in her home was immaculate. She also helped her daughter, Peggy, a fellow clean freak, keep all her nail holes clean too, not to mention the yards, garages and cellars of both houses. It wasn't a good idea to be in their vicinity when they were in a cleaning mood. You might find your bellybutton scrubbed out in an inattentive moment.

"Hi, Mom," Ed called as he got out of his car.

Her eyes lit up as she saw him, and she nimbly climbed down the ladder. "Hello, dear," she sang out. "How's my famous reporter son today?" Although her hair was prematurely white, Ruth Riley's smooth skin belied her fifty-some years. She was small and trim and could work rings around people half her age.

"Fine, Mom, just a little hungry. You got anything to eat?" She always had a refrigerator full of wonderful things to munch on.

"Not tonight, Eddie. Peggy and I cleaned it out this morning and threw all the leftovers away. If you wait until I'm finished here, I'll be happy to fix you dinner." She gave him a little bearhug, turned and headed for the ladder.

Ed grabbed her. If she escaped back up that ladder, she wouldn't quit until she had traveled around the whole house, leaving sparkling windows in her wake. "Hey Ma, I'll do the windows. You make me supper, okay?"

Doubt showed on her face. In her mind, Ed knew, only she or Peg could clean windows properly. Her son would leave streaks and spots and God knows what else. "If you're sure you can do a good job...." she trailed off uncertainly.

"Don't worry Ma, you'll think Peggy did it." He was hungry. He knew what they'd look like when he was done, but figured she had all day tomorrow to redo them. Besides, he would only have to wash a couple before she was finished. He climbed the ladder and she entered the kitchen.

Two hours later he was still shining glass. Every time Ed called in to see how she was doing, she said "Just fine," so he kept on spritzing and squeegying until every pane of glass winked slyly at him in the setting sun. He did a good job in spite of himself. She wouldn't have to redo these windows. Ed dragged into the kitchen and slumped into a chair.

"All done, Mom. What's to eat?" His arms hung leaden at his sides and his legs ached from clambering up and down the ladder. Annie and his mother had him ready to beg for mercy.

She smiled sweetly at him and replied, "Hot dogs, canned beans and a baked potato from the microwave. I hope you don't mind?"

"It took you two hours to make dogs and beans and zap a potato?" Ed sputtered, his arms flapping like wet rags in a strong breeze.

"Oh, no, dear, I had to clean the cupboard shelves and wash and wax the kitchen floor first."

"What!"

"My list for the day," she explained, "included the shelves and the floor. Maybe tomorrow I'll touch up what you missed on the windows."

Ed gave up. As hungry as he was, horse dung would have been delicious, and he gratefully wolfed down the dogs and beans with potato chaser.

Mrs. Riley chattered on about his newfound fame, managing to leap to her feet five times in an effort to find more in her immaculate refrigerator and cupboards to feed him. She reminded Ed she used to work in records for the county and that there was something about the Torrence farm purchase that was unusual, if it only would come back to her.

"Oh, I know!" she suddenly remembered. "Mr. Torrence paid cash he said he had won in a lottery for his farm. Not only that, it was in small bills. Everyone connected with the purchase was astonished, especially since it cost one hundred thousand dollars."

One hundred thousand dollars in small bills? What kind of lottery did he win, wondered Ed. "Are you sure?" he mumbled through the beans.

"Certainly I am. It's in the record at the courthouse, if you'll take the time to look. Mary Alice, the recording secretary at the time, wrote it in because it was so odd."

"Didn't anybody check into where he got that money?"

"I was told that that's what Mr. Torrence told the police chief when he was asked about it. Other than that, I don't know any more." Ruth wiped the tabletop around Ed's plate, picked up his glass and then the plate he was eating from and wiped under them, too. Ed ignored the action, having been through it a thousand times before.

"He told that story to Chief Wilson?" Ed asked in surprise. He found it impossible to believe Wilson would let a fishy statement like that swim by so easily.

"No. John Perth was sheriff then. He was a little old for the job, so he retired soon after." She started stacking the dishes in the sink.

"How old was he?" Ed responded like a latenight T.V. audience. He took the last bite of his mustard-laden hot dog and a swallow of milk.

She laughed and replied, "Eighty-three. Can

you imagine that? He was so popular, no one ever ran against him at election time, and things were always quiet in this town anyway, so he never had to work hard. His deputies did all the running around, I guess. He'd be shocked at what's happening now."

"That's a safe bet," Ed replied. "Well, Mom, I hate to eat and run, but I think I'm going to pass out. I'm beat."

Mrs. Riley accompanied Ed to his car while pressing the usual samples of mints, candies and packaged towelettes on him. As he drove off he could see her in his rear-view mirror pulling weeds from her grass as she worked her way back to the house.

Ed took the shortcut home. He didn't think he'd been to bed and asleep by nine-thirty p.m. since he was ten years old.

The following morning Ed walked into the Sheriff's office hoping to see Ben Gordon, and wondered if Ben had enjoyed his night in the slammer. Relatively speaking, it wasn't a bad little jailhouse, Ed mused. The cells of the jail were tucked away in an ell of the building in the rear. Each had a hard bunk, clean john and sink. What more could a convict ask for?

As Ed approached Willa Jean, the dispatcher, he noticed a stranger sitting on the waiting bench. He was wearing a tweedy, rumpled suit and a tie that was too wide. His shoes were "police" style but not shined. His seamed, sallow face didn't look too happy.

"Hi, Willa Jean. Who's the lost soul on the bench?"

She glanced at the disgruntled-looking man and replied, "He's from A.P. wire services. He says they picked up the double murders and want to cover them."

Ed brightened. A fellow newsman. "I want to talk to him. By the way, where's the Chief and his braves?"

She smiled and replied, "The Chief and the other deputies are out, but they should be in soon. Would you like to talk with them?"

"My God, no! I had enough of them yesterday. Did they tell you what they pulled on me?" Ed's face took on a pained look.

"They mentioned you were hitchhiking and told me to put it on the record. You shouldn't hitchhike, Eddie. It's a very dangerous thing to do, not to mention illegal."

"Tell me about it," Ed replied wryly. He turned to talk to the morose-looking out-of-towner slumped on the hard oak reception bench. He would be Ed's first personal contact with a big newspaper organization and he didn't want to blow it. "Hi," Ed said with a friendly smile and stuck out his hand. "I'm Ed Riley."

The stranger glanced at Ed's hand and then at him. "So what."

Ed stared at him a blink and then plowed on. "I'm the Town Telegraph reporter who broke the Torrence murder case." That should make this guy sit up and show some respect, thought Ed.

Still slouched, the stranger responded, "I read that little piece of garbage. Who ever told you that you could write?"

Stung, Ed snapped, "Who the hell do you think you are? That was a good story and you know it!"

"Oh, Christ," the stranger groaned. "I'm being punished for my sins. Last week I had to cover an overloaded garbage scow with no place to dump, and this week a couple of ho-hum murder cases in Lower Podunk. Go away, kid. You bore me."

"My pleasure," Ed growled back, and turned to Willa. He hoped that working a big paper didn't do that to everyone.

"Can I see Ben, Willa Jean?" He prayed she would say yes just to see the look on the A.P. reporter's ugly face.

"Heavens no, Eddie. Surely you know protocol only allows Ben's lawyer or the police to see him before he's released on bail, which of course isn't likely with two murder charges against him," and she sighed, shook her head and walked away.

Ed glanced at the reporter from the corner of his eye and wished he hadn't.

"You stupid kid, maybe you should learn the rules before you jump in the game," cracked the reporter. He "heehawed" a laugh at Ed.

"Ah, shut up, ratface," snarled Ed. "Go on back to the big city and run in your sewers."

The man leaped up, "Who're you calling "ratface," you babyface jerk. You should be sucking on pencils, not writing with them." He reached out and grabbed Ed's shirt.

Ed hauled back his fist and zeroed in on the reporter's nose. A great weight on his striking arm made him turn to see Willa Jean hanging on it. A second later the U.P. man got in the first and only blow of the discussion.

Chapter 13

Wilson strode through the door and glanced suspiciously around the front office. "What's going on?"

Everyone started talking at once.

"Shut up, all of you," he ordered. "What has happened here, Willa?"

She quickly filled him in, trying to keep her face straight as she spoke.

Wilson turned to Ed. "Riley, don't you ever get enough?"

Ed stood up, straightening his clothes, and thrust his chin at the out-of-towner, growling, "Nobody's going to come into my territory and treat me like dirt!"

"Looks as though he got a little on you, anyway," the Chief replied and shook his head in exasperation, noting the condition of Ed's clothes.

Wilson glanced at the other reporter. "You all right?"

"Yeah, the little snot couldn't hurt me." He straightened his shirt and tie.

"Do either of you want to press charges?" Wilson's tone suggested it was a lousy idea.

Ed shook his head in a negative reply while the stranger introduced himself to the Chief of Police.

"No, that's all right. Won't be the first time I've had to put some kid in his place." He held out his hand to Wilson. "I'm Joe Thorn from the A.P. wire services. You wouldn't mind answering a few questions, would you?"

"Maybe later," was Wilson's curt answer and he abruptly walked into his office and shut the door. It was common knowledge to those who knew him that Wilson never gave interviews, and apparent to the room's occupants the stranger had been pigeon-holed as a pain in the neck reporter.

Ed took grim satisfaction he wasn't the only newsman to be snubbed by Wilson.

Once again, Ed was leaving the stationhouse without doing what he came for. Not only that, each time had been a disaster. As he walked out the door, he glanced at Joe Thorn, who had returned to his hard bench along the wall, hoping to glean some information if he stuck around long enough. He noted that Thorn was surreptitiously waving goodbye to him with one finger. He returned the pleasantry.

It was also Ed's bad fortune to run into Wilson's daughter, Julie, as he left.

"Hello, Eddie. My, don't you look a mess." She gave him a mean smile.

"What's it to you?" He had had enough of her, too.

"Be a nice boy, Eddie, and maybe someday I'll let you visit me someplace where Daddy can't find us."

"Not a chance, Julie." He turned to go.

She slitted her eyes, grabbed his rumpled sleeve and spat back, "Insulting me is a bad mistake, you jerk. Don't forget the old saying."

"What's that?"

"Payback is a bitch!" She swept into the Sheriff's office.

Stupid bimbo, Ed thought as he strode down the street to the newspaper office.

He started making plans to poke around Lorenzo's house later that morning, but he had barely settled in at his scarred wooden desk when Mac changed his plans.

"Riley, get into my office," he bellowed down the length of the room.

Madge gave him a sympathetic look as he quickly maneuvered around the scattered desks toward Mac's door. Ted smiled at his typewriter and whistled a tune about a chain gang as Ed passed Ted's hallowed ground. A quick glance at his copy provided the ugly news that he was covering Gordon's arrest. Ted hadn't been involved in the event and yet he had the story. Something was seriously wrong. Alerted, Ed entered Mac's office.

"Hi, Chief. What's up?

With little hesitation, Mac plunged in. "Eddie, I'm going to yank you off these murder stories for a while."

"What?" Ed was floored. Mac couldn't possibly heard about the fracas at the police station already.

"Every time you go out that door something happens to you. Unfortunate things. We've decided you'd better lay low for a while and maybe the curse will wear off."

"We who?" Ed asked suspiciously, already pretty sure he knew the answer.

"Ted and I..."

"Ted? He wants my story! In fact, he wants all my stories. He's not concerned with my health. I could die tomorrow and all he'd do is steal the pencils from my desk."

"Well, I care about your health and you're not going to cover the Torrence affair for a while. Your mother would never forgive me if anything real bad happened to you." Mac clamped his jaw shut and quickly looked away.

"What's my mother got to do with this?" Ed challenged. "I'm a college grad with a year's newspaper experience under my belt, not a little kid running errands for you."

Mac sighed and gave Ed an apologetic look. "I promised your mother when you graduated from school I'd take you on and teach you the ropes, not get you killed."

"My mother? When did you and she get together and settle my future? Wasn't I hired on merit?"

Mac shifted around in his chair, rubbed his face with nervous fingers and glanced at Ed from under his bushy brows. "I guess she never told you about us."

Slightly dazed, Ed asked, "What are you talking about? Were you and my Mom an item?"

"Kind of," Mac replied.

"When?" Ed pressed.

"I guess it was in your junior year of college. She came to see me to find out what kind of racket you were getting into. At the time it was a pretty tame one." He cocked his head, giving Ed a wry smile. "But you've managed to inject a solid dose of danger into it, so she phoned me and asked to have you eased off the story."

"You tell my mother," Ed sputtered, "no, I'll tell my mother to butt the hell out, and I'm telling you, Mac, don't treat me like a five-year-old. Either I stay on this story or I walk. It's as simple as that." Ed charged out the door, slamming it behind him.

For the second time in his short career, he headed for Red's Place, a nearby bar that opened early for morning business.

This morning, Ed decided, he would join them, get loaded, go kick Ted's typewriter to pieces and then do the same to his mother's immaculate stove. He arrived just as Red, the owner, was unlocking the front door.

Red wasn't misnamed. He had bushy reddish-gray hair that had once flamed with color. His nose was lumpy and he had heavily seamed skin on his face and neck. He had run this bar ever since Ed could remember. Red's son, Ronnie, and Ed had been childhood pals and they had frequently spent time in the back kitchen of Red's sucking up colas and feasting on potato chips. Ron had since moved away to pursue his own interests.

"Red," Ed said as he shouldered his way through the barely open door.

"Hi, Eddie. What brings you here this early in the day?" Red replied in his smoke-graveled voice.

"Gimme a shot and a beer, Red. I'm celebrating." He leaned against the bar and cocked one foot on the brass footrail.

Red fiddled around the back bar searching out a particular bottle of liquor, one, Ed knew, he kept on hand for angry drinkers and troublemakers. He poured a short jigger of the special mix, and placed both the beer and whisky in front of Ed.

"Here Eddie, have one on the house and tell me what we're celebrating."

Ed grinned knowingly. "No, no, Red. Not the weak stuff. That's for sissies. C'mon, I'm paying for it. Give me a real belt."

Red sighed and shook his head, but complied with Ed's order. "First sign I see you're loaded, and you're shut off, no arguments. You got it?"

More hand holding, Ed thought, bitterly. Can't they realize I can take damn good care of myself. He squeezed out a smile at Red and replied, "Sure thing, buddy. I got it."

Red smiled back. "So what are we drinking to, Ed?"

"We're having a drink to celebrate the exposure of a conspiracy," Ed replied belligerently. He tossed down the whiskey. As it burned its way down his throat, he gasped and his eyes teared up. He grabbed for his beer and chugged it to wash down the little ball of fire. The flame was out, but he felt sick and leaned against the bar, his face pale and slick with sweat. "Jeeze, Red. When did you start serving moonshine?"

Red sighed and shook his head as he reached for the shot glass.

"Hey, put it back!" Ed snapped. "Pour me another and have one yourself."

"Ah, come on Eddie. You don't want this stuff."

"Red, my man," said Ed. "You are looking at a fellow, who, at the mature age of twenty-one is being conspired against by his mother, his boss and his co-workers. They all want me to sit behind a desk and write nice little stories about church socials and weddings. They don't want their little Eddie covering any nasty stories about a murder or two, or even a little shootout that's crummy with cops. No, not for their boy. Wrap him up in cotton. Keep him safe. By God, they're not going to get away with it." He slammed down his empty glass on the bar, shattering it. "Oh shoot, Red, I'm sorry."

"Yeah, it's all right, kid. You're having a tough time, and I'm sorry for you, but I'm only gonna sell you beer now, so don't get all nuts on me, okay?" He cleaned up the bits of glass.

"Hell, Red," Ed said contritely. "I wasn't going to wreck your place. I just feel like getting drunk."

"We'll see about that," Red replied with a smile, and he poured him another beer. "By the way, what do you know about that Miller farm escapade that didn't make it into the paper? Lots of local people in that mess."

"That's another one. I'm on the scene of a hot spot and good old Ted sucks up on it. I've about had it with the way Mac is handing my stuff over to Ted." Ed drank deeply from his glass and set it, with a clunk, back on the bar. "Fill 'er up, Red."

Red complied. "I mean, Ed, what exactly does Wilson know about the Posse? Anything you're not allowed to print?"

"Don't have any idea," Ed replied vaguely. "He wouldn't confide in me, anyway. Tell you what, though, there's a whole lot of drugs and guns floating around this area lately. I've got a hunch it's coming from the Posse judging from the stuff I saw on Wilson's desk the one time I got to snoop in there. I've gotta go to the library for more info. Maybe I'll do an in-depth piece on them. If they're going to be such a dangerous bunch, the folks of Portledge ought to know what they have to deal with. 'Nother one, Red." Ed pushed his glass across the bar. As he did, a new customer pushed the door open and scuffed over to a nearby barstool.

"Hello, Charlie," Red called out. "How're you this morning?"

Chapter 14

Ed had turned an antisocial shoulder to the new arrival as he entered, and Charlie, unaware of Ed's identity, slid onto the barstool.

"Did you hear the latest, Red?" he asked with a chuckle in his raspy voice.

"Naw. What's the latest, Charlie?"

"That kid reporter that's been running around the county looking for that crazy killer got in big trouble today!" He wheezed a laugh.

Red glanced at Ed and replied, "Yeah, how'd that happen?"

"Why, the durn fool got in a fight with some big city slicker newsman in Wilson's office and got himself thrown out." Charlie cackled and slurped his beer.

Ed saw the humor of it through Charlie's eyes and finally turned with a smile to the old man. "You know, you're right. It was a durn fool thing to do. But I wasn't thrown out. I walked out." He laughed at Charlie's surprise.

Charlie 'harrumpt' a few times, wiped his mouth with the back of his hand, then extended it to Ed. "Why, hello. It's sure a surprise seeing you here this morning."

"You never know where a reporter's going to

be, Charlie," Ed replied. "So what's new? Seen anything interesting next door lately?"

The old guy sucked on his beer a moment as Eddie and Red waited.

"Let's see," he replied as he cautiously checked the room. He leaned closer and said, "Last night, I thought I heard someone moving around in Lorenzo's, but I couldn't be too sure because the punks on the other side of the street were having a party. Loud music, ya know?"

Eddie and Red leaned in closer.

"Then," Charlie continued, "while I watched from my window, I thought I seen that same little twerp I saw the night Joey was croaked sneak along the fence and squeeze through a break in it. To tell the truth, it was so damn dark I mighta been seeing a dog. I was looking for ya at the newspaper office earlier to tell you, but they sent me off. Said they didn't know where you had got to. Good thing I stopped in here, huh, boy?"

Red turned to Ed and said with concern, "Sounds like your story is getting hotter by the minute, Ed. Maybe Mac is right. Better to be careful."

Irritated that another person was trying to bale him in cotton, Ed ordered another beer and grilled the old man.

"You saw the guy last night while Ben was in jail?"

"I think I saw someone," Charlie hedged. "It was awful dark, and lots of folks creep around in my neighborhood after dark."

"But you might have seen the same guy?" Ed pressed.

"That's why I come to see ya. It could've been the same one."

"Did you tell the police about it?" Red asked

Charlie as he sat a fresh beer in front of each man.

"Not me," the old man replied. "I ain't getting mixed up with no cops. I already been through all that with Eddie, here!"

"Just the same," replied Red, "If you don't tell the cops what you saw, you could be charged as an accessory."

"Ah, I still ain't sayin' nothin'," grumbled Charlie, and he took another swig of beer.

Red nodded, as if in agreement.

"Did you see anything else?" Ed asked.

"Naw, nothing," Charlie replied.

Having pumped Charlie dry, Ed ordered another glass of beer and faded into thought.

Obviously, if someone was still creeping around Lorenzo's house, it was a good possibility Ben wasn't Joey's killer, although he could be Mark's. What he couldn't come up with was a connection. While he pondered, he ordered another beer. As he drank, spilling some of it slightly, a stray possibility occurred to him.

Julie. She spent a lot of time at the farm, definitely not dressed for riding, and seemed to be pretty cozy with Mark. Did Joey kill Mark out of jealousy and then did someone else kill Joey over drugs? Pretty far-fetched. This town, like a lot of small towns, looked clean as a whistle on the top, but there was always a sub-layer of crime the citizens didn't like to acknowledge. Maybe one of Joey's buddies went nuts the other night and wacked him. Mark couldn't have been the only one around in the drug trade. That was a tidy solution. Ed's thoughts became fuzzier as the moments wore on.

"Hey, Eddie," Red called from the end of the bar. "Telephone."

Ed slurred, "Me? Tell them I'm not here."

"Sounds like work, Ed. You better take it."

Sullenly, Ed wondered how they had tracked him down. He stood up, lurched three steps to the left, another three to the right and stumbled into the barstools. Finally, he reached the phone. Red handed it to him, shaking his head.

"Something wrong, Red?"

"Not a thing, Eddie." Red retreated to the other end of the bar near Charlie, setting Ed's empty beer glass in the sink as he passed it.

"What?" Ed barked into the receiver.

"Is that you, Riley?" Mac asked.

"Yeah. What do you want?"

"I have a garden club reception for you to cover, but I'm beginning to think it's a bad idea. What the hell are you doing?"

"Having lunch! Where's the party? I'll handle it." Ed was damned if they'd take that away from him, too.

Mac replied, "Go ahead, Riley, but you'd better not screw it up. Here's the time and place."

Ed scrawled the information into his notepad, slammed the receiver onto the hook and swung around to face Red and Charlie. "It appears my presence is necessary at a high society garden party. If you'll excuse me, I'll be on my way." He weaved slightly toward the exit, dropping the price of his drinks on the bar as he passed.

"At least you still have your job, Eddie," Red called after him.

"Big frigging deal," Ed replied, slamming the door behind him.

Chapter 15

Ed drove the back streets through town, being careful to come to full stops at the signs, sometimes stopping even when there weren't any. The circuitous route finally took him to the city limits and the nearby entry to the country club. The Connequie Country Club represented the height of social acceptance in Portledge. If you hung out there for any reason, other than as an employee, of course, you had attained the rarefied air of the elite. Ed had never been invited yet. He laughed to think that Mac had sent him there for a garden society reception. Apparently, Mac must have reconsidered, for when Ed arrived, Marge, the society columnist, was in the parking lot waiting for him.

"Hello, Eddie," she trilled and hurried to his car.

"Why, hello to you, Marge. Who sprung you from the prison block?" He smiled up at her lopsidedly. "I thought you never left your desk come hell or high water."

"Mac realized you were way past flood stage after you hung up. Since I was the only person available at the time, he sent me here to take your place. I hope you don't mind?"

Ed slouched down in the seat and replied in a bitter tone, "I'm surprised it's you and not Ted. He's got all my other stories. Sorry to drag you out of the office. Guess I'll go home."

"Why don't you sit here in the shade and rest awhile? In your state you could cause an accident."

"I'm not too drunk to drive," he snorted. "I got out here, didn't I?"

"Yes, dear, but you look sleepy. Maybe a little nap would help." She reached across him and yanked the keys from the ignition. "See you later, Eddie."

Before he could react, she darted out of reach and trotted into the building.

"Shit," Ed muttered. He halfheartedly struggled with the door handle for a moment, then slid down on the seat and passed out.

Three hours later, the luncheon meeting over, the "Flora Club" members poured out of the building chattering about this begonia or that rose as they headed for their respective cars. Ed had forgotten that his mother was a member, a charter member at that. Before long, she strolled by Ed's car, deep in conversation with the Mayor's wife, Estelle Fraser.

As they passed near Ed's car, Estelle remarked to Mrs. Riley, "Ruth, isn't that your son's car?" Ed's car was unmistakable.

Both women turned back to look at the primer-spotted vehicle when a disheveled, blear-eyed Ed reared up in its front seat. He twisted around and found himself face to face with his mother.

"Hi, Mom," he whispered weakly then groaned and grabbed his head. The whole world was too bright and loud, including his own voice.

"Whew," gasped Estelle and flapped her hand in front of her nose. The rank odor of stale beer rolled in waves out the window at her and Mrs. Riley.

"My goodness," said Estelle. "What is it with these young people today? My husband, Mayor Fraser, says that ever since the fifties and sixties when Henry Longmeyer was mayor, society has just crumbled."

Ruth shot her a withering look, then turned her attention to her sodden chick. "My God, Ed, you're drunk!"

Retreat, he decided, was the only way out. Ed fumbled around to start the car and found the keys were missing. He could remember Marge taking them. "Where are the keys?" he groaned.

"Would you excuse us, Estelle?" Mrs. Riley asked, and she quickly sent her fellow club member away. She leaned through the open car window. "I could brain you!" she hissed into his ear. "You'd better explain yourself, young man."

The absurd vision of her and Mac in a clinch bobbed into his mind, and he hissed back, "I'll explain myself when you and my boss do the same. It's bad enough you wrangled this job for me, but now you want to tell him how I should do it, too."

"He told you?" Mrs. Riley asked, dismayed.

"Yeah, he told me." Ed stared belligerently at her.

Breathless, Marge arrived and glanced through the car window at Ed.

"Hi, Ruth. Eddie looks terrible, doesn't he?" She shook her head and smiled.

Mrs. Riley whipped around. "Marjorie, why didn't you tell me he was out here? Look at him! Just what is going on down at that paper? Every time I turn around, my son is being beaten or terrorized and now he's humiliated both of us with public drunkenness! Mac assured me that working for the Telegraph would be a nice safe learning experience, not an exercise in dangerous and stupid living."

"You're right, there," Marge agreed soberly. "None of us ever anticipated what's come about since Mark's death, least of all Mac. If it's any consolation to you, Mac took Eddie off the story this morning. I think that's what's caused his current condition." She leaned in the car window. "How're you feeling, Eddie?"

"Don't ask," Ed groaned. "Just give me back my keys!"

"What do you think, Ruth? Should we let him drive now?" Marge asked, a twinkle in her eye.

"Only if he agrees to go straight home," his mother replied angrily. "I'd like not to have to worry about him for the next few hours, anyway."

While the two women discussed his condition, Ed noticed Marlena coming out of the club. She was dressed to kill. "Hey, Ma, what's Marlena doing here?" he whispered, sudden curiosity dampening his current anger.

Mrs. Riley's expression softened. "Poor thing. I guess she's trying to start her life over since Mark's death. She was a member of the "Flora Club" a few years ago. She came today to renew her membership. She looks ill, doesn't she?"

Ill? Ed thought. Mark hasn't even been buried yet and she's starting her life over again? He decided to tail her in spite of how lousy he felt and see what there was to see.

"You're right, Ma. I'll leave right now so you don't have to worry about me. See you later." He grabbed the keys from Marge, started the engine and moaned as the noise set off, stabbing sparklers in his head.

The two women watched him pull away.

Marlena left the parking lot with a little spin of gravel, Ed directly behind her.

In spite of his best efforts, Ed couldn't keep up with the lead-footed Marlena. When he arrived in town he thought he had lost her for good. There were plenty of turnoffs, and more than likely she took one. Maybe he would follow his mother's order after all and just go home. It sounded like a great idea now. He was almost disappointed to find Marlena's car parked on the main drag, but he parked across and down the street from her. The afternoon sun beat down on his car. In a matter of minutes, Ed became nauseous and overwhelmed by the heat. He flung open the car door and staggered out onto the sidewalk.

Waxen faced, he leaned against the building with his eyes clenched shut, gasping for air. The rank fumes wafting off him kept the pedestrians as far from him as possible.

So much for concerned citizens, Ed thought as he fought down the urge to vomit. He didn't think he'd ever feel decent again.

"Looks like this one should be in the drunk tank, don't it, Chief?"

Ed opened his eyes to see Longmeyer and Chief Wilson staring at him. "Something I can do for you guys?" he asked, blearily.

"Let's run him in, Chief. Public intoxication," Longmeyer said with a laugh.

Chief Wilson elbowed Pollard out of the way. "You been drinking and driving, boy?"

"Absolutely not," Ed replied angrily. If they didn't catch him doing it, he sure as hell wasn't going to admit it.

"Well, you sure stink like it. What have you been doing?"

"Nothing illegal, if it's any of your business.

Now if you'll excuse me, I've got to leave." Ed saw Marlena leave the Darrell Anne dress shop and get into her car. She must be getting some new duds for her new life, he thought, and he pushed by Longmeyer and the Chief to follow her.

"You better watch what you're doing, kid, if you know what's good for you," Longmeyer shouted after him, as he watched Ed chase after Marlena.

Chief Wilson stood there with his arms crossed on his chest and a grim look on his face.

Ed's head was splitting and he battled with nausea as he pulled into traffic to catch up with Marlena. She didn't seem to be in much of a hurry as she turned left, then right on familiar streets. She parked too fast for Ed to pull in well to the rear, so he tried to ease by. Not an easy task with his high profile junker. With a little jolt he realized where they were. It was Jones' Funeral Home, the same one his father had been laid out in. First his father, now his father-figure in the same place. Ed suddenly felt sad and exhausted, and wanted only to go home. He drove around the corner and disappeared.

A glance in his rear-view mirror revealed Marlena shading her eyes, watching his retreat.

Chapter 16

Ed awoke after what seemed only moments to the pitch dark of a moonless night. As he lay there, he smelled something familiar. Where had he smelt it before, he wondered? It was so pleasant, so evocative of home, his mother's home. My God, he thought in a panic, am I in my mother's house? Ed sat bolt upright, jolts of lightning ripping through his brain. Gripping his head with both hands, he groaned, "I swear to God I'm never drinking again." As he sat waiting for the firestorm in his skull to subside, he reached over what he hoped was his bedside table to turn on a light. He was relieved to find himself in his own bedroom, but there something was wrong with it. Ed gazed around slowly, sniffing the air, and finally noticed the most telling clue. The spot on his nightstand where he had traced his initials in the dust was no longer autographed. The letters were obliterated. In their place was a reflective surface he could deter a vampire with.

"What the heck?" said Ed as he stumbled from bed and over his slippers which were neatly placed alongside. He looked at them, baffled. "Where did you come from?" He hadn't seen them in weeks. He gazed around the tidy room that reeked of pine cleaner and furniture wax. The smell nauseated him and drove him to the kitchen for some Pepto Bismol.

While rummaging through the refrigerator for the bottle, he realized that no one but his mother could have done all this. The whole place, including the refrigerator, was immaculate. Floors, countertops and tabletop gleamed with a waxed brilliance they hadn't seen since the day he had moved in. When did she do this, he wondered, irritated. He remembered the children's fairy tale where the sleeping shoemaker's work was being done in the night by some kind of gnomes or elves. "Same with Mom. She must have been here when I was passed out because the place sure was a mess when I came home. I'm going to have to get my house key back from her." He was slightly mollified when he discovered his mother's "cure-all"; a jar of homemade chicken soup she had left in his refrigerator.

After a quick meal of hot soup and a cold cola, Ed's anatomy was at full power again and he was ready to roll. He sat in the kitchen fiddling with his soup spoon wondering where he should roll to at one-thirty in the morning. He could try Billy's Bar, but decided one Pink Lady per lifetime was enough. Besides, the hardnoses that inhabited that joint wouldn't spill any information his way. Torrence's farm? No. Too long a drive tonight. Maybe, thought Ed, he would just park outside Lorenzo's house for a while to see if any mice were at play since the cat was dead.

By two a.m. he was parked across the street from Joey's house and rummaging around on the front seat for some of the sample gum that lay in the litter. He used penlight for aid. From where he was sitting he could see a portion of the backyard and the fence that blocked the backyard of this street of houses from the low income, three-story apartments behind them. He had hopes of spotting that mysterious little guy Charlie had seen creeping through the broken section in that six-foot wall.

Ed, too full of nervous energy to sit for more than a few minutes at a time, soon developed problems. First his back itched, then his feet. Then his legs fell asleep, and when he moved, millions of needles stabbed them like a demented acupuncturist. "It's going to be a long night," he muttered as he massaged his tingling limbs.

Ed was just rubbing a fresh bunch of pins out of his skin when a movement near Joey's house caught his eye. A small dark figure crept through the break in the fence and across the part of the yard Ed could see. He would never have noticed him except for the extreme blackness of the figure against the silver gleam of the wood in the moonlight. Once in the yard, the figure was barely visible.

Ed opened his door and shut it behind him with a gentle click, not worried about the courtesy light. He had smashed it one night during a playful moment with an old girlfriend. He crossed the street in a huddled, limping, crouch. The combination of numbness and needles in his legs had him half crippled. He stopped in the deep shadow of a tree to pound some life back into his tortured limbs.

His legs restored to working condition, Ed silently crept around the sides of the house, pausing at each corner and watching every bush for movement. He peered into the windows, one by one, along the way. His heart was pounding so loudly, he wondered that a neighbor didn't fling open a window and tell him to keep down the noise. The interior was pitch black, revealing nothing. Maybe, Ed thought, if I shine my penlight through the window, I might scare something up.

Ed aimed the flashlight into the room and flicked it on, directly into a masked face staring back at him. With a startled yelp, he leaped backwards, stumbled over a bush and fell on his back. At the same time, the black-clad figure bolted out the back door and raced across the lawn.

"Hey, you, stop!" Ed struggled to his feet and sprinted after the retreating runner.

The escapee barely looked back as he squeezed through the empty slat of the fence.

Ed reached the opening and tried unsuccessfully to cram himself through it too. Although Ed was slim, he was still too bulky to fit through the narrow opening. In desperation, he grabbed the top of the fence and clambered over, falling awkwardly to the other side. He squinted through the badly-lit area for the racing figure, but he was gone. Ed ran to the street and looked up and down but no one was visible. There wasn't even the sound of running feet, or the engine of an escaping vehicle, just the naked lawns and bare-bone buildings of the apartments.

Ed cursed as he started the long walk around the block to his car. His hand was on the door handle when he heard a raspy cackle of a laugh across the street.

"Nice job, Eddie. You look like we did in boot camp when we was running the obstacle course."

Ed looked across the street to see Charlie Smith in the dim light of a streetlamp sitting on his porch chaisse smoking a cigarette, flicking the ashes into the weeds that choked the front yard.

"Hello, Charlie. Had you ever considered being

a stake-out man for a P.I. firm?" Ed and Charlie laughed at Ed's lame joke as the reporter crossed the street to his best source of information.

"Did you happen to see what just happened?" Ed plopped down on the metal chaise glider next to the grinning oldster.

"Well, kiddo, I saw someone scare the crap outta you. Is that what you want to know?" Charlie wheezed a laugh through his smoke and took another drag.

Ed flushed a little at the barb. "He only startled me," he protested.

"Now, take it easy, Ed. I was only kiddin' with you. That guy would had given me the spooks, too. Gotta hand it to you, though. You gave one hell of a chase."

Charlie spent a lot of time on surveillance, considered Ed. I wonder what was going on around here before Joey died. Maybe I ought to jog Charlie's memory a little.

Ed slouched comfortably into the musty cushions of the chaise. "Yeah, I did a little track and high jumps in college. All that sitting around in class made me twitchy." Ed hoped he could establish a personal rapport and grease the information slide. "You seem like a guy who knows the score, Charlie. In the interests of running down both Mark's and Joey's killer, would you be willing to tell me all the rest of the stuff you won't tell the cops?" Ed leaned toward Charlie reassuringly. "I know you don't want to be involved, but you've seen my stories in the paper. Some of that information came from you. Did I ever implicate you in any way?"

"Nooo..." Charlie replied, "but some reporter guy named Joe Thorn came by today bugging me for information. Said it was off the record. But the minute I started to talk, he started to write it down in a little pad. 'Piss on that', I said to him. You're not getting me involved in no murder story." Charlie's eyebrows furrowed into an angry line.

"Joe Thorn! That guy's a weasel. He's the one who caused all the trouble in Wilson's office." Ed was furious that Thorn would come in and roil up Charlie. As far as he was concerned, Charlie was his personal informant, not to be shared with anyone.

"So, that was the guy who decked you, huh? How'd you let him do a thing like that?" Charlie seemed concerned at Ed's ineptness.

"Willa Jean grabbed onto my arm just as I started to swing. Thorn had a clear field." Ed touched the tender spot on his cheek at the memory. The pain on his face wasn't nearly as bad as that to his pride.

"Women," snorted Charlie.

Ed just smiled. More than likely Willa had saved him from a worse problem. At least when Wilson came in Thorn looked like the troublemaker instead of Ed.

"So, Charlie. Will you help me? I want to be in this business a long time, and the trust of my information sources is crucial." He sat tensely, waiting for Charlie's answer. This was new ground for Ed, and he didn't want to screw up the first informant opportunity of his burgeoning career.

"It's tough to be young and new on the job, ain't it, kiddo?" Charlie commiserated. "Tell you what I'm gonna do. I'm gonna give you the "hometown" benefit of the doubt. What I mean is, you and me gotta live here, and if you screw me over I can guarantee you won't get no more help from folks like me in this town. Sound fair?"

Ed was astonished. Was this the same seemingly simple old guy he'd known for two days who had already helped him considerably? "Gee, Charlie, of course it sounds fair, but why the threats?"

"Let's just say I seen and heard things lately that make me want to keep a closer eye on my skin."

Ed became jittery with excitement. "What things, Charlie? Tell me! I swear to God I won't tell a breathing soul where I heard it." He wanted to whip out his pad and pen to record everything, but the Joe Thorn incident kept his hands out of his pockets.

Charlie sighed heavily. "I'm gonna be sorry I'm telling you this. I feel it in my bones." But he lowered his voice, forcing Ed to lean in closer to hear him. "There's a bunch a' people in this neck of the woods that got a little thing going called the Posse. I first heard about it when I was hanging out in Red's place. He's a member, ya know. Now Red's a decent guy and don't cause no trouble, but some of the others got funny notions 'bout how far they can stretch the rules of this here group. Take it from me, they play rough."

"Like the blowup at Miller's farm the other night?" offered Ed.

"Yeah, like that. Now I ain't saying I know for sure that Lorenzo was a member, but I do know that I see guys, and sometimes women, I know are members of the Posse coming and going outta his house. Mark Torrence was one of them."

"No way," Ed breathed and leaned back limply. He couldn't picture Mark as one of those wild-eyed nutcases they hauled out of that house the other night. Mark was like a father to him. He couldn't possibly belong to that bunch.

"Are you sure, Charlie? Maybe Mark was there on some other business."

"Yeah, monkey business," agreed Charlie, sarcastically.

"And you say Red belongs, too."

"Told me he does, but he don't like most of the others. Too crazy, he said." Charlie suddenly grabbed Ed's sleeve, making him start. "You keep away from Red," he ordered. "He's my pal and I ain't gonna have you screwing that up. You got it?"

Ed was surprised at the strength of the old man's grip. "Hey, take it easy. Red's kid is my friend. I'm not going to get his dad into trouble. There's no law against belonging to an organization like the Posse."

Charlie relaxed into the cushions after patting Ed's arm. "I don't like to be that way, Ed, but a man has to protect his friends. But I guess you know that." He smiled reassuringly.

Ed smiled back. Now was not the time to say, 'if your friends are homicidal maniacs maybe you shouldn't protect them.' "You're right, Charlie. A man has to look out for his friends. And now that you've dropped a bombshell into my lap, is there anything else you can tell me?"

"That's about it, and I guess with Lorenzo gone, things will quiet down considerably next door." He rubbed his stubbly chin. "Gonna be kind of dull around here."

Ed stood to leave, reached out and shook Charlie's hand. "Not in this neighborhood." For as he had reached for the old man's hand, they both heard a man and woman cursing each other in a house down the street, the shouts sharply punctuated with smashing glass. "G'night, Charlie."

The following morning at the newspaper office, Ed gritted his teeth and called Wilson to tell him about his nocturnal adventure, omitting any reference to Charlie.

"Damn it all, Riley," Wilson bellowed over the vibrating line. "Can't you keep your nose clean for twenty-four hours? Every time I turn around, you're meddling where you don't belong! One more time, and I'm going to have an injunction served against you. That should stop you."

"You can't interfere with the freedom of the press, Chief," Ed snapped back. Managing to cope with the events of the past few days had gone a long way toward stiffening his spine against the onslaught of the Chief's temper.

"I don't want you messing around the crime scenes anymore, Riley. Keep the hell away, or I'm throwing you in jail!" Wilson slammed the phone in Ed's ear.

"Fuck you!" Ed screamed back into the dead phone, and quickly looked up to see several startled faces staring back at him. "Sorry," he muttered. Face flushed with embarrassment, he slid down in his seat.

Within seconds Mac strode down the aisle and planted his bulk firmly on Ed's desk. He picked up a pencil, tapped it on the desk's surface, then neatly snapped it in half. "We don't like language like that in this office, Eddie. You know that."

"Yes, sir," Ed replied in a near whisper.

"It won't happen again," Mac stated flatly.

"No, sir," said Ed, "but Wilson tried to tell me to stay out of the investigation."

"We've all told you to stay out of the investigation, now haven't we? What the hell an I going to do with you?" Mac paced a short path beside Ed's desk. "I'll tell you what. You're right to resent being taken off the Torrence story. Ruth and I were wrong about that, and I for one, am sorry. You can continue with the Torrence thing, but no covert investigating on your own, and you're to leave Lorenzo's death to Ted."

"What about the Posse story? I initiated that one, too."

"Ted finished up that one. It's old news. Just stick to Torrence and forget Joey."

"You know they're tied together, and still you won't let me handle both stories," Ed replied bitterly. Privately, he had a suspicion the Posse was mixed up in their deaths, but considering Mac's attitude, he wasn't about to let his boss hand that gem over to Ted, too.

"Let's just say I'm deflecting some of the danger onto Ted," Mac said.

"Yeah. Cold day in hell he'd make enough waves to splash himself," Ed said sarcastically.

"Maybe you could take a lesson from that," Mac answered angrily. "Now keep your language clean and yourself out of trouble while the Torrence investigation is going on. I'm tired of worrying about you!"

Ed watched glumly as Mac returned to his office. So quit worrying about me, he thought. Just because you dated my mother a few times doesn't make you my old man. After brooding a few more minutes, Ed picked up the previous day's paper, scanned the "Lorenzo" headlines and read the garden party article Marge had covered for him.

She did a nice job as usual, and had made a list of the ladies who had attended. Alphabetically, Marlena was toward the bottom.

Ed shook his head in disbelief. Marlena sure surprised him yesterday. She was sober, dressed and at the country club, all in one morning. Pretty light entertainment for a woman whose husband was just murdered. Not only that, she had shopped and had apparently taken care of Mark's funeral, too. Mark's death seemed to have energized her. I wonder if she could have squeezed through that fence? The picture of her voluptuous form hanging out the second story window came back, and with a laugh, Ed discarded that theory.

He glanced at the clock. If he moved fast enough, he would have time to make a round trip to the farm for a human interest interview with Marlena, a cozy chat with Annie, the heartless, and maybe, when no one was looking, he could have a peek inside Ben's cabin. No doubt Wilson and company had already examined it, but he'd like to take a look for himself.

Stealthily, Ed made for the exit door when Ted called out.

"Hey, Riley. Don't sneak out without an assignment." He arrogantly raised his eyebrows and smiled, his lank frame draped comfortably in his padded office chair.

"Crap," Ed whispered, careful not to offend nearby ears, and traveled back through the labyrinth of desks to the assignment board. Under his name was one listing. Mac had decided that this morning Ed was best utilized at the Morningside Daycare Center for an interview with the children about a play they were staging and the actual viewing of the play itself. He turned to see Ted snickering into his typewriter. Ed glared into Mac's office windows and yelled, "I'm going to cover this big story now! See you later." But Mac wouldn't look up, not even when Ed slammed the door on his way out.

Chapter 17

Ed stopped at his office's equipment department, which consisted of one gunmetal gray wall cabinet in the layout department. He unlocked it, pulled out a clipboard and signed out a camera with a telephoto lens, then carefully placed it and several cans of film into a sturdy black carrying case. The idea of long distance spying appealed to him, particularly since close up spying had become so damaging to his person.

Fortunately, the daycare center assignment was not as bad as Ed had anticipated. The morning went swiftly and the kids were a lot more fun than he thought they'd be. The play was a riot. Of course, it wasn't supposed to be and many faces in the audience were twisting in a tortuous effort to quell outright guffaws. He was having the same problem, himself. Ed took a few pictures, shook a gaggle of hands, then beat it out of there. The pictures were turned in and the story typed by one p.m. Fortunately, Ted wasn't there to harass him and Mac ignored him, which made his getaway from the office much easier.

Ed drove the spine-breaking back road to the rear of Torrences' farm, parked his car and began the furtive trek up a low hill that overlooked the farmyard area. He had ridden there many times with Annie and sometimes with Mark to enjoy the view. Today, the view was as nice as ever, but nothing much was stirring down around the barns. Occasionally, Ed saw Annie or Marlena walking from the barn or the arena with a horse or alone. At one point, Marlena went into the house and came out wearing a dress. She got into the car and left, but Ed noted she was headed toward town. He figured she was going to the funeral home, someplace he would go before the day was over. To pass the time, he took a few snaps of the buildings and the women. He enjoyed zeroing in on unsuspecting subjects with the telephoto lens. As he finished the roll of film and was concentrating on putting a new one in the camera, he heard a faint click behind him. As he turned to look, he felt the side of his head explode.

Ed groped his way up from a blackstrap molasses pit. This time someone was pressing his head with what felt like a brick, really a soft cloth. He could hear conversation.

"Thank goodness you happened along, Officer Longmeyer," Annie gasped. "He could have died!"

"Well, he won't, will he? The ambulance should be here in a couple minutes," returned Longmeyer's nasal whine. "Riley's got a head as hard as granite. If the fool would mind his own business he wouldn't get hurt."

Ed painfully hefted himself onto his elbows, turned his head to see who the speakers were and was rewarded with the frightened face of Annie on one side and the sour one of Longmeyer on the other. Ed, unfortunately for Longmeyer, involuntarily chose that moment to vomit on the deputy's shoes, then he collapsed onto the ground.

"What in hell are you doing?" yelled the officer.

"Puke in the grass, you jerk!" He stamped the toes of his brogans on the grass, then pulled some broadleaf weeds to wipe the remaining mess away.

Annie leaped back, startling the horse she had ridden there. She collected herself, returned to Ed and anxiously examined his bloody head.

"I hope that ambulance gets here soon," she said to Longmeyer. "This head wound looks bad."

"Who cares," he yelled angrily. "When Wilson assigned me to watch your place, he didn't mention I might have to deal with a gunshot, vomiting, snoopy reporter." He continued to vigorously rub his shoes with the grass.

Annie looked down at Ed to hide her amusement and stuffed her jacket under his head. "You poor dumb klutz," she crooned. "Who did this to you?"

Ed smiled back vaguely and wondered where she had learned a foreign language.

"Always in the wrong place at the wrong time, aren't you?" She gently dabbed at the blood on Ed's face with the cloth, but only managed to smear it around. By the time the ambulance arrived a few minutes later, Ed's face resembled a pizza. Annie relinquished her possession of him to the paramedics. Longmeyer continued whining in the background about his shoes.

When the ambulance had arrived, Chief Wilson, along with the county crime investigation unit, had pulled up, too. The investigators started staking yellow ribbon around the scene and Wilson took a look at Ed as the paramedics gave the unconscious reporter emergency treatment.

"What have we got here?" he asked the medical personnel as he craned his neck for a good look at Ed's bloody head.

"Bullet wound," the busy medic replied and

pressed a compress against Ed's skull while her partner inserted a needle to start a drip into Ed's arm.

"Can you tell me anything else?" The Chief's face was set in harsh, angry lines.

"Yeah," she replied as they loaded up the now unconscious Riley. "Another quarter inch to the right and we'd be scooping his brains off the ground." She slammed the ambulance's back door behind her and seconds later hauled Ed off to the hospital.

Wilson, accompanied by two state policemen, interrupted Longmeyer, who was still scraping his shoes clean. "What did you find when you arrived?"

"I saw little Miss Morris kneeling by Riley swabbing the jerk's head. Guess if I hadn't been patrolling that road down there Riley would've been a goner." He glanced down the hill to the unusually smooth dirt road that ran at the base of the hill. "By the time she could have gotten to the house and called for help, the kid might have died." Longmeyer smiled, showing yellowed teeth behind thin lips.

"Be careful, Myron," the Chief remonstrated. "Someone might think you did it just for the fun of it."

"I wouldn't waste a good bullet on him," hooted Longmeyer.

Wilson shook his head at his deputy, then joined Annie.

"Annie," he greeted and touched the brim of his hat.

She nodded in reply.

"I'd like to hear your version of this event."

"It's very simple," she replied. "I was riding Bandito in the outdoor arena when I heard a popping sound, just one, by the way. It's a good thing

I was looking up the hill at the time or I would never have seen Eddie sort of hop up and then collapse. I rode up here as fast as I could and found Ed lying in the grass, his head all bloody." She stared him directly in the face as if to challenge him on the veracity of her story.

"When did Officer Longmeyer appear?" he asked.

"He drove up a couple minutes after I reached Eddie. Good thing, too. It would have taken me a long time to get to the barn to make a call."

"So he called it in right away?" The Chief watched her intently.

"Oh, yeah," she agreed. "I yelled down the hill to him and he got on the horn right away." Then she laughed. "Eddie rewarded him by barfing on his shoes."

Wilson suppressed a smile. "That's all I need for now. I think the state men want to speak to you, too."

"Do you think Ed will be okay? I know he can be a pain in the butt, but I really like him." Worry showed plainly on her face.

"Don't even think about it," Wilson replied in a fatherly way and gingerly patted her shoulder. "I think it would take a bazooka to cave in Eddie Riley's hard head." He smiled at her and stepped back as the state investigators approached Annie for questioning.

The reassurance seemed to help her, for she squared her shoulders and looked less frightened as the others arrived.

The afternoon wore on, full of activity as a result of Ed's gunshot wound, but he was oblivious to it all. He was having an extraterrestrial experience.

LEAD A DEAD HORSE TO WATER 133

Ed dreamed he was traveling in a tunnel of blue light. Strange humanoid shapes with pale blob faces hovered over him, encasing his mouth and nose in plastic and wrapping him in space age fabric. Finally, he lunged from the tunnel to a brighter one, surrounded by ghost-like creatures draped with loops of tubes. They kept shouting at him and pinched him painfully, "Can you hear us, Mr. Riley? Do you feel this, Mr. Riley?"

"Leave me alone," Ed yelled. "Get away from me!" He struggled against their invasive hands.

"He's showing signs of consciousness, Doctor," one of the aliens called over its shoulder. "He's moving his limbs and whispering something."

Gradually, Ed managed to focus on a familiar face and smiled weakly through blood-caked lips. "Hi, Doc," he croaked. "Nice to see you again."

Dr. Edders frowned at him. "You've gone and gotten yourself shot, Ed. You'll have to stay with us a few days."

Shot? Someone has shot me? "Like hell!" said Ed, weakly, as he struggled to sit up. "I've got to find out who shot me. The S.O.B. has one coming.

As Ed ranted, Doctor Edders and a nurse gently pressured him back onto the table to continue treating his head wound.

"Shut up, Riley!" snapped a hoarse voice that cut through the din. Officer Pollard joined the medical people with Ed and glared down at him.

Surprised, Ed momentarily clammed up. He stared up at Pollard, then recovered his usual brashness. "I might shut up for Wilson, but not for you," but he kept quiet anyway. Talking had become a huge effort.

"What's it take to get you off this case?" snapped Pollard. "You're only supposed to report the news, not make it."

Ed began laughing in a tittering, squeaky fashion.

An incredulous Pollard asked, "What the hell's wrong with him?"

"Nerves," explained Dr. Edders. "He needs a few days' rest and treatment. A gunshot wound to the head and the emotional trauma he's been through have pretty well finished him off. Why don't you leave while we settle him down? Perhaps you can talk to him later when he's more collected." The doctor gently prodded the heavyset officer toward the door and escorted him out while Ed giggled hysterically in the background.

The four days Ed spent in the hospital seemed endless to him, and for the first time since Mark died he felt a little afraid. Being shot at was no small thing. Staying here was a drag, though, he griped to himself and anyone else who happened to be in the room. He lay staring at the ceiling, plotting out stratagems to leave the hospital unnoticed, but a strange lethargy dragged at him, confining him to trips to the toilet or daily forced marches with a nurse in the hallway. Chief Wilson provided the most entertainment when he stalked into Ed's hospital room the second day of his confinement to give him the third degree.

He gazed down at the pasty-faced Eddie. "You did it again, kid," he said gruffly. "Aren't you getting tired of this?"

Wilson looked so uncomfortable Ed laughed weakly and said, "To tell you the truth, Chief, I think I'm cured of my curiosity. Garden parties and grade school plays look mighty appealing to a man in my condition."

Wilson signed with apparent relief and rubbed the back of his neck with his hand. "Good. Now I won't have to wonder what you're up to and worry about what shape you'll be in when I see you."

Stern again, Wilson interrogated Ed. "What were you doing on that hill, Ed? I thought we understood you were to back off."

"Look, Chief, I'm sorry if I make your job harder, but you have to understand Mark was like a father to me. I couldn't leave this alone any more than you can. I have to admit, though, these guys are playing too damn rough, and I don't think Mark would want me dead on his account."

"I'm glad you feel that way, Eddie. Now, can you remember if you heard or saw anything before you were shot? Anything at all?"

Lying there, looking up at Wilson, Ed would have liked to help the man out, but the awful truth was that he couldn't. "I'm sorry again, Chief, but I can't remember a damned thing from the moment I laid down on the hill to watch the farm. Total blank." Ed shrugged his shoulders in apology.

"Oh, come on, Riley. You must remember something," Wilson replied sarcastically.

A wisecrack leaped to Ed's lips, but as he opened his mouth, a lifesaving miracle in the form of a nurse bustled to his bedside, jammed a thermometer in his mouth and told him, "No talking."

Wilson shook his head in exasperation and turned for the door, but pivoted back to Ed just before he left the room. "By the way, Ed, Marlena Torrence came in this morning and made Ben Gordon's bail. The only reason I'm telling you this is that despite your momentary disinterest in crime investigation, I've got a hunch you'll sneak back to it before long, and I don't want you going after him behind my back. I want you to keep away from him." Before Ed could spit out the thermometer, Wilson was gone. Ed struggled to sit up, but the nurse firmly pushed him onto the bed. "You just lie back down, young man, and keep your lips wrapped around this little stick. I'm going to get your temperature even if I have to tie you up and put this item in a more personal place to do it." She shoved the thermometer back into his mouth.

Appalled at the possibility, Ed lay still while she finished checking his body heat and blood pressure.

Marlena and Ben! It had to be them. Ben was little and Mar was nuts! They were the perfect pair to kill Mark and move drugs. Ed's damaged head wrestled with the concept while he twisted this way and that on the hard surface of the bed.

Ed's mother and sister kept guard over him as long as the nurses would let them stay. They tidied the room incessantly and brought him boxes and jars of special food. By the third day he'd gotten well enough to resent their coddling, but by the fourth day he had had it up to his stitches.

Ed groaned in exasperation when they walked into the room. "Mom, Peg! I can't take this anymore," he snapped. "Everyone on the floor is laughing at the circus you're putting on."

"Come on, honey, people don't laugh at mothers who take care of their children. Besides, this way I can keep a close eye on you so you don't sneak out the door to get into more trouble." She gently removed his pillows, plumped and replaced them.

Peggy added, "Look at the good side, Eddie. At least with guards like us, your old bean will stay intact for a little while." Both women smiled down on him like two mother hens determined to keep their attack-prone chick from harm.

"Just leave," he growled. "I'll be fine." He tried to fend them off as they started straightening the bedcovers.

Dr. Edders briskly walked through the door and smiled at the two women who hovered so devotedly over their captive. "Morning all. How's our patient?" He examined Ed's head and peered into his eyes with an instrument while the women gave him a rundown on every meal Ed had eaten and every temperature fluctuation since he had been admitted. Ed flushed with embarrassment as they talked. Dr. Edders looked at him and winked. "This young man looks fit to travel today." To Ed he sternly added, "Another head injury like this, young man, and you'll be doing fingerpaints for entertainment. Give yourself a rest. The police are doing their best to find who shot you, so you needn't bother flinging yourself back into the fray." He waved goodbye as he stuffed his stethoscope into his coat pocket and quickly left the room.

Ruth and Peg immediately emptied Ed's closet, packed his bag they'd brought in for this occasion and stood expectantly, waiting for him to dress.

Ed waited too, finally realizing they thought he would dress with them in the room. "How old am I, two? Get out of here! I can dress myself just fine." He clutched the covers to his chest in defense of a sudden military charge on their part.

"Well, jeeze, Ed. It's not like I'd never seen you before," Peg laughed, then hooked her arm through her mother's and they made a gracious exit.

Ed wasn't aware that they stood close to his door just in case.

Chapter 18

The ride home from the hospital with his mother and sister added to Ed's headache. For twenty minutes they chattered about his car.

"You'll never recognize it now," his mother declared. "Peg and I cleaned it inside and out."

"That's right," Peg added. "No more trash on the seats. No mud caked on the doors and mats." She took every opportunity to chide Ed about his slovenly habits, today being no exception.

"Oh, thanks," said Ed insincerely. He hated it when they took over his life, but he was still having a rough time combating it. Between the two of them, they had ruled him since infancy, and the habit of knuckling under was a tough one to break. He was sick and tired of it. One day soon he'd revolt, but not today. Today, he was just sick and tired.

The women bustled Ed upstairs to his apartment. Barely civil to the clucking hens, he walked unsteadily to his bedroom, locked the door, shucked his clothes and crawled between the lightly scented, cool, ironed sheets his mother had made the bed up with that morning. There were some benefits in his family's perpetual harassment, he thought as he burrowed down and pulled the covers over his head. He could hear them moving around in the other room, and he wondered what they could possibly find to clean.

After enjoying the cool crisp sheets a few minutes, he called Mac to let him know he was out of the hospital and available to work.

Mac cleared his throat. "Just want you to know you don't have to come in tomorrow morning. Take the rest of the week off, too. When you come back on Monday, we'll discuss assignments and see if any changes need to be made."

Before Ed could squawk, "What changes?" the line was dead. Changes, huh? Changes could be good, he reasoned, or bad. He got a crummy feeling the school play circuit was going to be his exclusive ground for one hell of a long time. Before the murders occurred it would have been okay, a learning experience, but now, everything else paled. He could still hear the women in the other room. It sounded like they were wrecking the place, but there was no way he was going to unlock his bedroom door. He invited them to leave.

"Hey, Mom, Peggy! You can leave any time now." His shout pierced the walls, he knew, because the man next door promptly banged on the wall with what sounded like the heel of a shoe.

"Okay, Ed. We'll be gone soon," came the faint reply.

But it wouldn't have mattered how long they had stayed, for in a matter of a few minutes, he was sound asleep.

Ed looked at his clock-radio and twitched the window curtain aside beside his bed to be blinded by the morning sun rising above the roof of the house across the street. He realized he had slept for over twenty hours. Gently, he fingered the bandage taped across the side of his skull and winced. Ed gingerly slid out of bed and carefully walked around his bedroom, fingers trailing the furniture and walls for balance. The brief unsteadiness passed, and except for the thumping head pain, he didn't feel too bad.

He wandered out of his bedroom and was irritated to find the livingroom completely rearranged. He immediately changed it back to the original placement despite the fact that the women's floor plan was much better. It didn't do his condition any good, but the satisfaction of thwarting some of their controlling efforts did. He took a sparkling dish from an immaculate cupboard and had a bowl of fresh cornflakes (as opposed to the usual stale cereal that sat in open boxes on the kitchen counter). After spending twenty minutes lounging in his tatty, overstuffed recliner contemplating the peeling paint on the lofty ten-foot ceilings, the peace and quiet palled. Sticking around the apartment didn't get the job of catching the bad guys done, and he was determined to nail Mark's killer. Even after several days, the police still hadn't made an arrest, and now he, too, had been the target of a murder attempt. The memory of the report on Wilson's desk recurred; a huge cache of assault weapons like AK 47's and Czech Vz58's were found at Miller's farm after the Posse shootout. According to Charlie, Mark belonged to the Posse, but Ed had a hard time picturing his instructor wielding an assault weapon in a standoff with the cops. Maybe Mark wanted to resign from the increasingly wild-eyed bunch, but found himself in the bad position of knowing too much. Man, this is just like a bad movie, Ed thought. Sitting there with a bandage on his head, he wished it were, and that he could leave the theater and find Mark still alive. Well, Mark wasn't, he thought angrily, and he was going to do something about it right now! No sitting around whining over a little "flesh wound." Another trip to Torrence's farm was in order.

He made a brief call to his mother to assure her he would be spending the afternoon in bed and didn't want to be disturbed. A pop-in visit on her or Peg's part was now neatly averted. The phone was still warm from Ed's hand as he drove away hoping he would be able to return under his own steam. He missed the clutter of condiments, snacks and small implements that had littered his front seat and kept reaching for the now absent gum or toothpicks. Annoyed at Annie, Ed wondered why he hadn't heard from her. She didn't visit or call on him in the hospital. Considering how long they'd known each other and that she had been right there when he was shot, she had a little explaining to do, he thought. He saw her approach as he parked near the barn. As she got closer, he noted her step lacked its usual spring, and her face looked drawn and tired.

"Eddie! Am I glad to see you! How's the head?" She reached up to touch his bandage.

Ed drew back in alarm. "Don't touch! It hurts."

"Oops, sorry." She grabbed his arm and pulled him through the open barn door, and propelled him toward the hay chute.

"Hey, wait a minute," Ed protested as she handed him some work gloves and a small knife for cutting hay bale string. "What do you think you're doing?"

"Look, Ed," Annie stated flatly, "with Mark dead and Ben unavailable, I'm shorthanded as hell. All of our staff has left, and Marlena has suddenly discovered a social life at the country club, so whenever an even partially able-bodied person pulls up this driveway, I put him, or her, to work."

Ed wasn't about to tell her he couldn't handle it. "Can we at least talk while we're feeding the horses?" This was not turning out the way he wanted.

"Sure. I'll water them. You can give them their hay."

"I'm sorry I missed Mark's funeral, Annie. How did it go?"

Annie shook her head as she filled a bucket with water. "You wouldn't believe the people who showed up; business people connected to the farm, students, townspeople. I saw Chief Wilson, Longmeyer and Pollard, but there was an odd-looking bunch, too. Sort of paramilitary types, fatigues and all. Marlena was pretty cozy with them. Even Longmeyer was there and talking with them."

"Fatigues, huh." I guess they were making sure Mark was dead, Ed thought bitterly. "At least a lot of people showed up to pay their last respects. I'm glad of that. Speaking of last respects, how come you never visited me at the hospital while I was more than half dead?" he complained as he shook apart another hay leaf into a manger. The effort made his head swim.

Annie paused and gave him a wry look before replying. "I don't have any time for things that aren't life threatening, and since they said you'd live, I figured I'd see you here sometime soon. You can never stay away, even with Mark dead. So what's the attraction now?"

"You've gotta be kidding! I get repeatedly beaned because I'm digging into Mark's murder and you wonder why I'm here. C'mon Annie, you can't be that dense."

"I think you're wasting your time," she replied.

"Chief Wilson will root out the killer before too long. Why don't you keep out of his way and quit interfering." Annie angrily splashed water into the stall bucket, startling the horse within.

"What're you so mad about?"

"Maybe you worry me," Annie replied without looking at him. "Maybe I don't want anything to happen to you." She hurried to the next aisle.

Whoa! There's first base, Ed thought excitedly, and he shook hay into the mangers with nervous hands.

"Thanks, Eddie," Annie said as they finished. "You cut my work in half. Now that the horses are settled, why don't you and I have a snack at my place?" Without waiting for an answer, she walked out of the barn, Ed hurrying after her, yanking the work gloves off his hands.

He weaved slightly as he tried to keep pace with her rapid walk to the small, one bedroom cottage she occupied on the farm. It had a similar mate where Ben lived ten feet further up the gravel drive.

She waved him to a seat at the kitchen table as she strode straight into the bathroom. Ed collapsed more than sat at the tidy table in the small but immaculate room and idly wondered how she managed to keep the place so nice with all she had to do.

The walls were painted a pale yellow with small flowers stenciled here and there in natural-looking drifts. Ed liked the effect. He glanced around at the old but nicely refinished cabinets and counters. Even the Danish modern sofa and chairs, which had to be thirty years old, were clean and conveniently placed. No clutter or grime was evident anywhere.

This girl has a lot in common with Mom and

Peg. Maybe I'm making a mistake here, Ed thought. She might be a big pain in the neck, too.

Annie emerged from the bathroom, leaned against the doorjamb and looked carefully at Ed. "I think chocolate milk and sugar cookies would hit the spot. How about you?"

"Cookies and milk?" This was a wholesome approach. "Sure, anything that's handy suits me fine."

"Where did you get these?" Ed asked as he stuffed the sixth three-inch cookie into his mouth.

"Baked them myself late last night. It relaxes me after a tough day. You seem a little sleepy. Would you like to lay down?" A look of concern crossed her face at his pasty visage.

Ed, groggy from the recent exertion and a now full stomach, glanced into her feminine bedroom. "Will you join me?"

Annie laughed. "Go lay down before you fall down." She strode from the cottage, refreshed and ready for several more hours of work.

Batting zero, he wistfully mused as he made his way to her bed and, with a soft groan, lay down.

When Ed awoke, the cottage was quiet except for the purring of a large orange cat curled at his side. Ed raised up slightly to listen for Annie. Disturbed, the cat yawned, stretched and gently sank its claws into Ed's side.

"Ouch!" Ed yelled as he jerked back. He shoved the cat away from his lacerated skin. "I'm glad I wasn't naked," he grumbled as he stood in front of Annie's dressing mirror. He pulled off his teeshirt to see eight pinpricks of blood ooze from his side, grabbed a scarf off the dresser and wiped his skin clean. Pressing the blood-smeared cloth to himself, Ed stalked to the bathroom to search through the medicine cabinet for antiseptic. He swabbed it on the punctures, visions of catscratch fever in his mind.

"Damn cat. Why'd Annie let that thing in here?" he muttered as he rinsed the scarf and hung it over the shower rod. It was best not to leave a mess if he wanted to be invited back. Ed was about to leave the cottage when something about the scarf struck him. He wandered back to take a closer look at it.

"Well, I'll be a...," he said, pulling the yellow and black striped cloth off the rod. "Lorenzo's scarf, or one just like it. Where the hell did Annie get it?" Ed held it up to the light as though to read the answer in the weave, then rehung it on the rod.

He dressed and went outside to find Annie.

She hadn't gone far. She was in the outdoor arena working a school horse. With so few students since Mark's murder, the animals had to be exercised daily.

Ed leaned against the fence and watched as she walked in a tight circle holding one end of the long lunge line that was attached to the halter of the horse trotting in a larger circle around her.

Annie smiled at him. "Feeling better?" She gently flicked the long tail of the whip at the horse's back feet as he sensed her inattention and tried to slow down.

"Feeling wounded," he replied and propped his elbows on the fence. "Your gargantuan house cat affectionately sank his claws into me."

As Annie again snaked the long whip at the horse's heels to remind him what they were there for, she said with a wicked grin, "Yeah, I should have warned you about him. He doesn't like to be disturbed when he's smack up against you and cozy. Sorry about that. Did you find some antiseptic?" She clucked encouragement to the horse who was shaking his head in protest as if to say "talk or work, but don't do both."

"Yeah, I did. I found a nice yellow and black scarf too. It's too bad I had to use it on my wounds. Where'd you get it?" Ed tried to keep the inquisitorial tone from his voice, but somehow, it leaked through.

Annie halted the horse and eyed Ed angrily. "All of a sudden I feel like a suspect, Eddie. Just what is it you're getting at?"

"That's not what I meant. It's just that the scarf in your house looks exactly like the one Joey Lorenzo wore the night he broke into my apartment. So, I wondered how you could have one too." He flushed with embarrassment.

Mindful of the steaming horse, Annie set him at a cooling walk. "Julie Wilson gave me the scarf after I had admired it on her. She said she had several and didn't mind parting with one, and, no, I don't know why she had so many of the same kind."

"I'm sorry," Ed replied. "Guess the head injuries have made me wacky. What can I do to make it up to you?" Annie's explanation seemed plausible, considered Ed, but generosity had never been Julie's style except when it came to causing trouble. Then she was openhanded to a fault, he reflected ruefully.

"I'll tell you what, keep me supplied in horses until dusk, then I'll let you off the hook. Ben isn't around this evening, and don't ask me where because I don't know that, either. With your help I should be able to finish these critters by suppertime. Bring me Sally next. Toby here is about done."

"Okay," Ed agreed contritely, and went to the barn for the horse she asked for.

Poor Annie. Neither Marlena nor Ben seemed particularly interested in doing the necessary work around the farm these days. Marlena's efforts were hit or miss at best and God only knew what Ben was up to. Well, I'll do what I can for her this evening, Ed thought, and maybe after dark I'll scope the place. Apparently, there's something in the house someone wants pretty badly. It could be Ben, who probably wouldn't harm Marlena, or it could be one of Mark's fellow Posse members. In which case, Marlena was in big trouble. They played rough.

In a few minutes he had Sally on a short lead and started his penitent work.

Chapter 19

As soon as the last horse was exercised, cooled and put to bed, Ed escaped the farm to go home. Annie didn't offer any supper and he wouldn't have accepted. He just wanted to get the hell away before she found more for him to do. His head was killing him.

His apartment looked mighty good to him as Ed keyed open the door and stepped inside, happy to see that there were no mom-made "improvements" perpetrated during the day. He showered and changed clothes; something in basic black was perfect for an after-dark affair. The clutter in the kitchen was returning, he noted with satisfaction as he added the evening meal's crockery and pans. The television kept Ed company through dinner and the remainder of the evening while he watched the news, then napped through some game shows and sitcoms. Ed leaped awake when a fat lady leering in closeup on the T.V. set screamed, "What do you think you're doing, you moron?" He checked his wrist watch and was relieved to find it was only eight forty-five p.m. It was also a blessing to find the pain in his head had mostly disappeared, too. He popped a couple of mints into his mouth and trotted down the steps to his car.

In the last light of the day, his brain clicked on autopilot during the trip to the farm and he thought about Annie. Was she a murderess? It seemed more likely that Joey, rather than Julie, had handed out that scarf. Joey and Annie? The mix was as palatable as grease and milk. Ed steered off the road half a mile from the farm, parked it under a clump of trees and fervently hoped he could get it back out when the time came.

From over the low hills a sliver of moon had risen slyly to join a wash of stars and it cast a faint trace of light over the landscape. Ed zigzagged like a commando across the hummocked field to the border of the farm. A final quick sprint brought him to the far corner of the paddock where, panting, he crouched by the fence and considered his next move. I should go home, he thought as he rested his head against the post. The ache had emphatically returned, plus a case of shivers feverishly washed over him. Maybe I just should have told Wilson about the scarf instead of coming out here, alone, where someone had already died.

"I'm doing it again," he whispered to the indifferent stars, and he girded himself for a long night.

After mulling over the possibilities, Ed decided to creep into the deep shadow of the barn and keep an eye on possible developments. Like himself, the murderer seemed to like the night shift. He edged along the fence to the corner of the barn and got a nasty jolt when a cat unexpectedly rubbed against him. Ed froze in a crouch, puffing slightly, until his heart shifted out of racing gear, then he crept into the blackest area of the barn's shadow and settled down to wait. The cat was ecstatic for the company and purred like a thunderstorm when she curled up on Ed's lap, expecting to be petted. He repeatedly pushed her away only to have her crawl back. He thought of flinging her into the next county, but canceled the urge. Better a purring cat than a screeching one. Both Ed and his captor settled in for the duration.

The night was warm. As time wore on Ed fought leaden eyelids, but the monotonous hum of the cat's purring gently lulled him into sleep.

"Crack! Crack, crack!" split the night. Ed leaped up, spilling the yowling cat from his lap and looked wildly around for the sound's direction. After heartbeat's silence, a crash came from Marlena's house, catapulting Ed toward it. As he raced across the parking area, he struck against a running figure just coming around the garage away from the house, but before he could react, Marlena flung open her door and started shooting a pistol at him. Ed plowed into the ground, scraping his face and ripping his shirt in the process. The intruder bolted out of sight toward the barn.

"Marlena, it's me, Ed Riley. Quit shooting, for God's sake!"

"Eddie," she shouted hoarsely, "where the hell are you?"

"I'm lying here with my face in the dirt, you trigger-happy maniac."

"Get in here," she held open the door, "before that nut gets you."

He shakily arose and slipped by her into the house. She slammed the door behind him and stuffed the small gun into the pocket of her bathrobe.

The kitchen was transformed. The chaos of the past was gone. In its place was order and spotlessness except for a pile of broken dishes on the floor. "What happened here?" he asked. For a moment he wasn't sure if he meant the metamorphosis of the room or the craziness that just took place.

Marlena sat down hard on a chair, grabbed her cigarettes from the table and lit one. After taking a deep drag she said fiercely, "That same son-of-a-bitch that was in here right after Mark died came back tonight, but I was ready for him. He no sooner crawled in through the livingroom window when I went after him, but the creep got away. You got in my way, or I'da plugged him."

"You okay?" His eyes swept her for damage.

"No. Just a little rattled. Speaking of night visitors, what the hell are you doing here in the middle of the night? Weren't you ordered to stop skulking around?" She contemplated him through narrowed eyes. "One of these days your nosey habits are going to get you into big trouble."

"I'd say they already have," Ed replied, grinning.

"Did it every occur to you that you've been trespassing every time you snuck around here spying on the place?" Marlena cocked her head back, cigarette smoke curling around her face like dirty gauze.

Angered, Ed sputtered, "I always came and went as I pleased when Mark was here."

"Yeah, well, Mark isn't here anymore, is he? From now on, you check with me before you decide to sneak around," she ordered. "Now sit down. I need some company I recognize for awhile. We'll have some coffee and then you're going home." She scuffed in ragged slippers to the cupboard and dug around for cups.

Ed didn't like Marlena's edict. It conflicted with his notion of investigative reporting. "How the hell can I help find Mark's murderer if I have to announce my comings and goings to you?" Angrily, Ed clutched the back of a chair, his knuckles white.

"Not all of them, sweetie. Just when you're coming out here."

Ed sat down silently as she poured the coffee and reached in the refrigerator for the milk. Although he knew she was within her rights, the thought of letting her know when he was on the farm alarmed him. She could be one of the guiltiest parts of this mess. He sure didn't want her to know when he was staking out the place. He stirred milk and two teaspoons of sugar into his coffee. It was time to change the subject.

"Mar, a while back you told me Mark fixed a lottery, but didn't win much. Are you sure about that? Maybe he won big, but didn't tell you. After all," he continued, smug with his knowledge, "Mark paid cash for the farm without battling an eye."

Marlena stiffened. "How did you know that?"

"My mom worked in county records at the time and she said that's what he did, and in small bills too. Weird, don't you think?"

Marlena shifted restlessly in her chair, fumbling with her spoon. "I know Mark paid cash for this place, but I am positive there was no more money from the lottery afterward. He used up all the winnings."

Ed wasn't convinced she was telling the truth.

She continued, "At any rate, what business is it of yours if there was money left over? If it exists, it's mine."

Ed stared at the coffee grounds at the bottom of his cup, wishing instead they were tea leaves that predicted a rosy future. What he saw was: paramilitary types in fatigues at Mark's funeral; Red, of Red's place, with an AK 47 stashed in the back room; Annie, sporting a fancy bandanna, whacking a guy's throat with a silver-handled knife; and Marlena shooting a pistol at him every chance she got. They call this feeling "paranoia," he thought, and was suddenly anxious to have Wilson on the premises. Looking up at her, he said, "Marlena, you'd better call the cops. The screwball you chased out of the house was probably the killer."

"Okay, Ed. Whatever you say." Casually, she reached for the wall phone, put the receiver to her ear, glanced toward the window and shrieked.

Ed whipped around to face, he was certain, a deranged gunman. Staring back were two long narrow faces with large, glowing eyes. Ed leaped up, knocking over his chair, and the ugly face at the window snorted and jerked back. They could hear hooves thundering away.

"Damn it all!" Marlena screamed. "The horses are loose." She flung herself out the door to Annie's cottage. "Annie!" She pounded on the door. "The horses are running loose. Get out here now!" She whirled away to round them up.

Struggling into her jeans, Annie lurched out the cottage door, hair bedraggled and eyes bleary.

Ed had lagged behind slightly.

She glanced at him and grinned. "Aren't I a sight?" She ran off after the faint echo of hooves as the school horses galloped down the road.

Ed knew he should run after the animals too, but he couldn't resist a quick search of Annie's place for the black clothing Marlena's recent unwanted guest had been wearing. He picked up a shirt and pants from her bed and held them up against the faint light coming through the window. They were a light print blouse and greenish-colored jeans. A glance into the tiny bathroom revealed the incriminating scarf was still hanging on the shower bar. From far off he heard his name being called.

"Eddie, get your butt over here and help us!"

He smiled. Marlena issued orders like a Marine drill instructor.

Only somewhat satisfied that there were no black clothes in Annie's bedroom, he left the cottage and trotted down the road to the commanding voice.

"Here," ordered Marlena as she handed over a rope with a horse at the other end. "Take this witch to her stall and lock it. Annie and I can handle the others."

"How'd you catch them so fast?" Ed asked.

"They never go far," she said. "Once we catch Rita, this one, the rest fall in line. Good, here's Annie with the rest."

Before long, the horses were bedded down in their stalls and three tired people straggled to the back door of Marlena's house.

"We still have to call the cops," Ed reminded Marlena.

"Why?" Annie sounded anxious.

"Look, Ed," replied Marlena, "it's one o'clock in the morning, and I have to get up early. Let's let this latest episode slide until morning, okay? I've had enough of reporters crawling around the place and interrogations from stupid cops to last me a lifetime."

"Oh, yeah," he replied, grinning. "Did the A.P. guy, Joe Thorn, show up here?"

Marlena curled her lip. "Yes, he did, but I had him on the run in five minutes, the jerk. He can move real fast when drinking glasses are shattering on him."

Ed laughed uproariously.

"Would someone fill me in?" Annie insisted. "Has there been some other disaster besides the horses tonight?"

Both Ed and Marlena looked at her in disbelief.

"You didn't hear the shots?" they asked in unison.

"No, I didn't," Annie replied, clearly irritated.

"Marlena took some potshots at someone tonight, myself included," Ed added wryly.

"And you aren't going to tell Wilson?" Annie asked incredulously.

"Not 'till the morning," Marlena answered. "He and his dopey crew will keep us up all night, and I've got things to do tomorrow that don't call for a groggy head. Now good night, and Eddie that means you, too." She entered her house, slamming the door behind her.

Yeah, right, thought Ed belligerently at the solid thump of the door in his face.

"Well, Ed," Annie said, "You've got your walking papers. Guess you'd better toddle along, and I'll be seeing you around. 'Night." She too went into her cottage.

He turned down the driveway trailed by a small pride of cats that had gathered during the conversation. "Scram, kitties," he hissed as he neared the street, and reluctantly they scattered, leaving him to walk down the dark road alone.

"I don't care what Marlena wants, I'm telling Wilson tonight about what happened here," he muttered to himself. "I'd rather have him pissed at me for snooping than homicidal for not reporting this A.S.A.P."

Ed was gratified when his normally cantankerous car started on the first try and backed out of the woods without stalling. He drove his rattletrap to town, its headlights painting a bright path before it.

Chapter 20

Ed parked directly in front of the police office in the forbidden zone reserved only for patrol cars, and glanced through the brightly-lit window to see Wilson's head bob across the upper portion of the painted pane of glass. For a while he just sat there, resting his head against the cushion, eyes closed, and felt his stomach grind in protest of the interview to come. Finally, reluctantly, he left the haven of his car and entered the building.

Ed squinted against the office's day-glow tubular light. "Hello, Chief," he said, and waited tensely for the anticipated negative reaction. The policeman didn't disappoint him.

"Well, if it isn't Eddie "The Perpetual Headache" Riley joining me in the middle of the night. Why aren't I surprised?" The grimace on Wilson's face only faintly resembled a smile.

Ed smiled back weakly. "You warned me to fill you in on the latest developments, so here I am."

"It couldn't be too exciting or your head would be bleeding." Wilson eyed him carefully. "So what's the latest?"

"Before I tell you, I'd like to know how the investigation on my gunshot head is doing."

"It's doing," the Chief replied crisply.

"That's it, huh? It's doing. Swell, just swell. I get shot, and you don't give a damn."

"Shut up, Ed," Wilson snapped. "I told you as much as I'm going to, so just back off!"

"Thanks a lot. It's nice to know things are going so well." Resentment against their one-sided arrangement roiled like magma in his gut. One of these days, Ed vowed, Wilson and he were going to rewrite these little scenes they enacted, and he was going to come out on top. Disgusted, he rapped out the evening's events, and particularly mentioned seeing the yellow scarf at Annie's place along with its connection to Joey Lorenzo. Try as he might, he couldn't shake his lingering suspicion of her.

"Don't worry about the scarf, Riley. Julie got a dozen of those for her birthday from her Aunt Mae, and she handed them out to anybody who would take one. Your girlfriend's off the hook." Wilson sat heavily in his chair. "Listen, kid. Go on home, dream about women or a Pulitzer and forget about tonight. This police department will take care of it in the morning."

Ed opened his mouth to protest, but Wilson fastened an iron-willed stare on him that steered Ed backwards from the room and out the station door. As he left the building, he realized Wilson hadn't crawled all over him about sticking his nose into the "Torrence" business again. Either the Chief was awfully tired, or he had washed his hands of him. Could be, Ed thought, Wilson hoped he would be the next victim. As he turned to go down the steps to his car, he bumped into Longmeyer.

"Oops, sorry, Myron," he apologized and tried to sidestep the scowling deputy.

"Real typical, Riley. You never watch where you're going."

"Aren't any of you low-rent cops ever civil?" Ed asked angrily. "All you guys behave like the Nazi Gestapo most of the time."

Longmeyer drew himself up to his full height of five feet, six inches, immediately reminding Ed of a kitchen matchstick, and replied proudly, "I'll have you know I come from a fine German family. In fact, if you'll recall, my grandfather Henry Longmeyer was mayor of this town for eight years. I'd say my antecedents were of a much finer cloth than your booze-sodden cretins."

Ed was momentarily stunned. It soon passed. "You son-of-a-bitch!" he yelled, and leaped for Myron's skeletal form.

He jolted to a stop, grabbed by Wilson, who had stepped through the door, catching both the last of Longmeyer's remarks and Ed in mid-air.

"Myron, please step inside," Wilson said through tight lips. Ed thrashed about in his hard grip.

Longmeyer hesitated, red blotches on his furious face. "I want to charge him with assault, Chief. The police are sacrosanct. He can't get away with this." His voice rose to a piggish squeal.

"Let me at him!" Ed yelled. "I'll crush that ugly spider! Nobody's gonna talk about my dad that way."

"No one is pressing any charges. Myron, get inside."

Longmeyer entered the station. The panes of glass rattled in the front door as he slammed it behind him.

Wilson finally had to put a headlock on the raging Riley. "Ed, simmer down!"

Ed had to stop struggling. The lock Wilson had on him cut his breathing and he was getting faint. After a few seconds Wilson released Ed, who sagged to his knees and sucked air raggedly into his lungs.

"You going to behave now?" Wilson stood over Ed, tensed for the younger man's next move.

"He shouldn't dump on my father. He couldn't help he was sick." Ed slowly stood up, rubbing the back of his neck where Wilson's police academy ring had pressed against the vertebrae.

"Well, you're both even then, because he's touchy as hell about negative comments concerning anything German. His grandfather was from there originally and drummed a strong sense of Germanic pride into him."

"I don't give a damn. He was born in Portledge just like me. He'd better get his loyalties straight." Ed glanced at his watch and asked tiredly, "Can I go now? I'm real sick of today. I'd like to get some sleep and see if tomorrow will be any better."

Wilson suppressed a smile. "Yeah, hit the road, Riley," and in a rare attempt at humor, he added, "but not the cops."

A tiny smile flitted across Ed's face at the briefly human police chief. "Okay, I get the message."

At home, Ed lay wide-eyed in bed unable to sleep. For the first time in a long while, memories of his father kept him awake.

It felt good being back at his desk, thought Ed cheerfully as he rummaged through the cluttered drawers. In his enforced absence, he had forgotten what was in them. Nothing exciting; pencil stubs, paper litter, a couple of college journalism textbooks and stale candy bars. Just like his front car seat. He turned to stare out the window into the faint light of a sun barely edging over the buildings.

Even after last night, he wasn't surprised to have crawled out of the sack so early. He had lain

160 SCHEURING

in bed like a board until he finally dozed off, then twisted, turned and thrashed the sheets right off the bed. His dreams were bizarre. The Chief had become a lion tamer, flinging Ed into the big cat's mouth to reward it, tempting it to do even more dangerous tricks. When the lion grabbed Ed, it turned into Annie. She choked him and stuffed him full of straw. He woke up in a sweat at 5:00 a.m., rushed through a quick shower and bolted for the Town Telegraph. Pawing through the garbage in his desk palled and, slightly sleepy, Ed cradled his head in his arms on its surface.

It seemed only a moment later when Mac shook Ed's shoulder. "Wake up, kid. What the hell are you doing here so early? It's only seven-thirty."

Ed jerked awake. He mumbled thickly in confusion, looking into Mac's curious face. He rubbed his eyes and slumped deeper into his chair. "Wilson was feeding me to the lions."

"You're a mess, kid. What's going on?"

Ed relayed the evening.

More people had arrived at the office, staring curiously at him.

"Well, well. The boy wonder is back," declared Ted. "I wonder what new adventures he'll enthrall us with now." He looked around to see if he had amused the staff.

Ted's seniority earned him a return smile from everyone except Marge, who outranked him by three years.

She bustled up to Ed. "Hi honey. How are you feeling?"

"I'm okay, Marge. I just wish Ted would fall into the printing presses."

"Now, now, don't be that way. You been here nine months and have had more happen in that little bit of time than Ted's had in twenty years. You can't blame him for being jealous."

"Jealous?" Ed sighed. "I'd be glad to let him experience my bullet wound if he'd like."

Marge laughed, patted him on the shoulder and returned to her desk.

Mac, still standing by, cleared his throat. "Here's the thing, Ed. You're still on light duty, but since you were involved in last night's fracas, and it doesn't seem to be a part of Lorenzo's death, I'm going to let you write it up on your byline. Enjoy."

Mac didn't get two steps from the desk before Ed had paper in the typewriter and was pounding away. He never saw the sour look Ted sent in Mac's direction.

Within a hour Ed had his story written and on Mac's desk.

Mac spent a few minutes scanning it, then tossed it back on his desk. "Okay. Drop it off on the proofreader's desk on your way to your next assignment."

Here we go, thought Ed. Back to reporting on the latest litter of kittens in town or, with any luck, it'll be an in-depth piece on the new sewer system. He forced a smile and waited.

"There are a lot of interesting people in this county, Eddie. I want you to hunt them up and do a story for our paper on them one at a time. Make sure you get their written consent and get a picture, too." Mac leaned back in his overburdened chair.

At first Ed couldn't believe his ears. Who gave a shit about the goofballs living around here? Ah, but wait, was this covert permission to investigate further into Mark's and Joey's death behind Ted's back? With a sly smile, Ed rubbed the side of his nose, winked and replied, "Sure thing, boss." He sauntered from the office, oblivious to the worried scowl on Mac's face.

Chapter 21

Ed was elated at the free hand Mac dealt him. The license to roam around and question anyone he liked was like being handed the keys to the city, and immediately wondered if anyone was ever really handed "the keys of a city." This is close enough to satisfy me, Ed thought, jubilant. "Stick to the town's more reputable people," was Mac's only rule. Why would I want to interview Bob and Mary Bland when someone like Charlie might be a thousand times more interesting? Old guys always had oddball stories about the past to relate, but no one ever took the time to listen and record them. The old folks died and took their histories with them. Ah, what the heck. He'd interview Charlie and sneak the story in sometime. Meanwhile, the respectable people would have a few minutes of small town fame.

The hours dragged by as Ed forced himself to interview what turned out to be what he considered some very boring people. Around six-thirty he sat in the local diner eating dinner, yakking with the waitress and watching traffic, noting with interest that not only were the Portledge police out in force, a couple of state cop cars were cruising the street, too.

"Hey, Millie, what's with all the cops tonight?" Ed figured she might know. Waitresses overheard plenty.

Millie glanced out the window as she sat a piece of apple pie in front of him. She proceeded to wipe the table where his other dishes had been and said quietly, "You didn't hear this from me, but a certain fat cop was here this afternoon in this very booth having a Superburger. He mentioned there was something big going down tonight. He got shushed big time by his boss."

Ed and Millie smiled at each other. They both knew who had the big appetite and mouth in the police department, and there was only one boss. "Thanks, Millie. I'll remember you in my will."

"Just remember me when you tip," she replied, and gave the table one more swipe as she left.

A little after eight p.m., Ed decided it was time to visit Charlie. He dropped a five dollar bill on the table by his empty pie plate as he left.

Ed knocked at Charlie's shabby back door and idly picked at peeling paint on the doorjamb as he waited. A country and western song wailed its sad message within. After a few minutes of renovation he knocked again and called, "Charlie, hey Charlie, you've got company."

From somewhere in the house Charlie yelled back, "Keep yer shirt on. I ain't deaf."

As usual, Charlie was the picture of sartorial splendor: the burn holes in his stained teeshirt, grease spatters on his baggy pants and his ripped-out slippers showed ragged toenails peeking through.

"Well, if it ain't the newsboy. You come to collect on the bill?" Charlie cackled. "Come on in, kid. You're sure a sight for these old eyes. I thought you was finished off for sure after your last fracas, but I see you're back for more." He opened the torn screen door and practically dragged Ed inside.

"I want to talk to you about yourself for a profile piece in the newspaper. How would you like that?" Ed asked as he looked around for a place to sit.

Charlie shoved a sleeping cat off a nearby kitchen chair and motioned Ed toward it. "What do you want to bother with an old fart like me?" he asked, tossing yet another cat off a second chair he chose. "You want a beer?"

"Sure," Ed replied, and allowed the recently evicted cat onto his lap.

"It's in the fridge. Get me one while you're at it."

In a few moments they were settled down, men and cats, working on the interview. Charlie seemed happy to cooperate. He glossed over his childhood, but when he reached World War II, the stories of danger and glory poured out of him, as Ed rapidly scribbled notes onto a yellow legal pad. Charlie's wartime experiences had been apex of his life.

"You've got some great stories, Charlie," Ed said, "but I need some proof. You got any?"

"Sure, boy." Charlie scuffed from the room. In a few moments, he returned carrying a shabby shoebox. It looked as though it had been handled hundreds of times. "Look here."

Charlie showed Ed old news clippings and photos that lay carelessly heaped in the box featuring himself receiving medals of various types. Underneath the yellowed paper, though, were neatly placed boxes which Charlie reverently removed from the shoebox and sat in front of Ed. One by one Charlie opened them, explaining the significance of each brightly shining metal disk, each with its own distinctive ribbon.

Ed smiled in admiration at the war veteran. "You're a genuine American hero," Ed congratulated. "Just wait until Mac gets a load of this." He started shuffling his notes together.

"Sorry, son. I can't let you do it. You ain't allowed to print a word of that stuff I just told you."

"What! Are you nuts?" Ed leaped from his chair, knocking it over and tumbling the cat onto the floor. Damn it! Why hadn't he gotten a signed release before he'd started? "Charlie, you'll have parades in your honor. A statue in the park! Why can't I run this story?" But the stricken expression on Charlie's face put the brakes on his anger.

The tousled old man looked down in embarrassment and replied, "I shoulda never told you any of that stuff, 'cause one thing I did canceled out all the rest, and I ain't never been able to live it down."

"What could have been so bad that you have to hide your medals in a cardboard box the rest of your life?" Ed righted the chair and sat back down. The cat stayed in the corner it had retreated to, keeping a cautious eye on Ed. The remainder of Ed's anger drained at Charlie's obvious distress.

Charlie sighed and stared at his hands as he rubbed the knurled fingers together. "I'll tell you, but you ain't gonna like it and if it ever gets out a lot of lives and reputations will be ruined. You gotta promise me you won't write this down anywhere, or tell anyone, ever. I'm trusting you, boy."

Ed, struck by Charlie's serious manner, sat down. "I'm honored that you trust me, but if it's that bad, are you sure you should?" He hated to pass up the rest of the story, but didn't want to take advantage of the man's confidence in him.

"I can't hold it inside no longer. I gotta tell somebody." Hands trembling, Charlie reached back into the box and pulled out a last piece of paper and shoved it roughly across the table. Ed picked it up and stared at it.

"A dishonorable discharge? How the hell could you get this after all the terrific commendations?"

"Commendations don't hold water against a major screw up. Got to be real careful of who you piss off in this world, sonny, real careful."

"What happened, Charlie?"

Charlie signed heavily and painfully, and began. "I was a demolition man, you see, and one night I was working with another soldier to blow a bridge. Real secret stuff. Only me and him and a colonel knew about it. I showed the guy where and how to set his charges 'cause I was the expert. So we set them all and waited for a passel of Germans that was supposed to cross over the bridge just before dawn. Well, it was pea soup that morning on account of the heavy fog and those people came marching down the hill to cross over. They crossed over all right...right to hell. We blew the bridge and all those folks sky-high and then skedaddled. Didn't even look back." Charlie paused, reluctant to continue.

"It sounds okay to me so far," Ed prompted. "What was wrong?"

"Turns out it wasn't soldiers we blew up." Charlie paused; a wracking sigh shook him. "It was refugees. Women and kids and old men trying to get the hell out of the war zone. The soldiers, Americans, were about twenty minutes behind them."

Ed was stunned. They sat there in silence as Charlie hugged his arms to his chest and slowly shook his head.

A reluctant Ed finally asked the question that hung off the tip of his tongue. "How could you make such a mistake?"

LEAD A DEAD HORSE TO WATER 167

"We were set up," groaned the shattered old man, watery tears traveling the crooked seams in his face. "The colonel turned out to be a fake. A picture of the real colonel was mailed to headquarters during the investigation but by then the faker had disappeared. Even so, the brass didn't want us around no more, so they court-martialled us, and we were drummed out."

"God, Charlie, what a lousy end to a great career, but what did you mean by reputations being ruined if the story got out?"

Charlie shifted uncomfortable in his seat. "I shouldn't be telling you this, being as you're a reporter and all, but I gotta tell someone before I pass on." He leaned toward Ed conspiratorially. "The other soldier's name was Longmeister, Hank Longmeister. About ten years after the war he showed up in town, strutting around, dressed to kill and money to burn."

"No! I'll bet he was glad to see you, an old army buddy and all."

"Tell ya the truth, I didn't recognize him at first. He'd got fat, grew a mustache and, get this, he changed his name." Charlie sat back and eyed Ed.

"For Christ's sake, Charlie, don't stop now. What the hell was his name?" Ed gripped the table in anticipation.

"Henry Longmeyer."

"Henry Longmeyer, the mayor in the late fifties, early sixties? Deputy Longmeyer's grandfather?" Ed was dumbfounded.

"The same," Charlie affirmed. "He must have changed his name so's he could get a fresh start. Me, I just hid on the wrong side of the tracks. Now you see why I can't tell any of the good stuff. Even though Longmeyer's dead his family would suffer. Anyway, no one around here knows about me, and

I'd just as soon keep it that way."

For once, Ed was at a loss for words. Nothing about Charlie had prepared him for the evening's revelations. He fingered the medals lying on the table and thought about Deputy Longmeyer's grandfather, the mayor his mother had often referred to as "Old Moneybags." She always said he dressed too well and had too much pocket change for a small town politician.

"Tell me, Charlie, did Longmeyer ever seem to have a lot of money when he was in the service?" Ed assumed that since they had been in the same company they had known each other for a while.

"I dunno. I never knew anything about him. He transferred into our unit just before the bridge job and always kept to himself. A loner."

Ed got a bad feeling about Mayor Longmeyer. The colonel was a fake. Maybe Longmeister was brought into the company just for the purpose of blowing the bridge and his court-martial didn't matter. He was going to bolt, anyway.

"Do you suppose Longmeister could have been a part of the plan and all that cash was part of a Nazi payoff?"

"Gotta tell you, son, it could be, and that military crap musta rubbed off on his grandkid, Myron, cause I heard a rumor at Red's that he was a radical member of the Posse. You know, those goofs that shot it out with the county police and state troopers the other night. Talk like that could cause big trouble for a deputy sheriff."

"I didn't know that," Ed replied, shocked. He thought back to that night and remembered he didn't see Longmeyer with the Chief and Pollard.

"Lots you don't know about the so-called "decent" folks in this burg. Sit around with me in the bars sometime. You might learn something."

Charlie yawned, stretched and gave Ed a weak smile. "Time for me to pack it in, kid, though I probably won't be able to sleep after digging up my lousy past. Now you remember, not a word of this to anyone. Promise?"

"Yeah, I promise," Ed replied, although that was the last thing he wanted to do. This Longmeyer story was too good to suppress. But Charlie trusted him, and maybe someday the truth of that event could emerge and he'd receive the honors due him. Ed thought about it while Charlie boxed up his war memorabilia. Gradually, Ed noticed one of the cats. Its attention was riveted on something outside. Stealthily it crept toward the door, tail tip twitching.

"Hey, Charlie," Ed whispered. "Do you have mice? Look at your cat."

Charlie stepped to the door to let the predator out. "Dang cats are always naggin' to go out....Hey!"

Just as he unlatched the small hook lock, the door burst open and Deputy Longmeyer bulled his way in. "Back up and no funny business, you creeps!" he ordered as he aimed his .38 service pistol at both men. "Close the curtains, old man." He kicked the kitchen door shut behind him.

Ed quickly raised his hands. This was a Longmeyer he had never known, but now, according to Charlie, might be the real deal.

The deputy kept both men covered with his weapon, but he focused on Charlie. "So, you knew my grandfather, and now you also know what a hero he was to the Third Reich."

Anger sparked Charlie's eyes. "He was in on it, wasn't he, him and the colonel. They shoulda hung the S.O.B.!" A shred of the fighting soldier flared up and he grabbed the iron skillet off the stove.

Longmeyer fired his pistol, striking Charlie in

his upper right chest. Blood spattered in all directions as the old man slammed backward against the wall and slid, unconscious, to the floor.

"You bastard!" Ed screamed and scrambled to Charlie. "You've killed him!" He frantically looked around for something to pack against the chest wound, but abruptly quit when Longmeyer placed the muzzle of the gun to Ed's head.

"C'mon, asshole, we're getting out of here." He yanked Ed up by his shirt collar and forced him to the door. Longmeyer quickly reconnoitered the street. The noise of the shot had already caused neighbors to turn on their porch lights and stand outside. Longmeyer flicked off the kitchen lights and dragged Ed out the door, across the dark porch and down the steps.

"Get your keys out. We're taking your car." With the muzzle of his pistol jammed in Ed's back, Longmeyer shoved him across the passenger side and into the driving seat.

Chapter 22

Hands shaking, Ed fumbled with the keys as he attempted to start the car.

"Hurry up," Longmeyer snarled. "Since you're so friggin' brave, you shouldn't be having such a problem."

Ed had no reply. It was all he could do to get the car underway.

Longmeyer gestured with his gun. "Drive toward Berk's Tavern, jerk."

"And then what?" Like a badly trained dog, Ed tended to forget his lessons within a few minutes, and Charlie's unfortunate encounter with Longmeyer was over the time limit.

"Shut up and drive, Riley." Longmeyer dug the muzzle of the gun into Ed's upper arm.

"I'm going where you want so quit bruising the merchandise."

Longmeyer laughed, a bit madly, Ed thought, and leaned back, apparently enjoying Ed's discomfort. The crackle of papers and boxes on the seat caught his attention.

"What is this crap? It's like a garbage can in here." He sifted his free hand through the clutter.

"Just stuff my mom gives me," Ed replied. Mrs. Riley had left a fresh supply to make up for what Peg had shoveled out.

"How sweet. Mama's little boy. C'mon, mama's boy, pick up the speed. Ah, there's the tavern. No, don't turn off. Keep driving, and when we reach Torrence's farm, pull in."

The farm again. Everything happened there. In spite of his fear, his curiosity demanded satisfaction.

"What could you possibly want at the farm, Deputy? There's nothing left there but horses."

Once again Longmeyer dug the gun into Ed's arm. "None of your frigging business."

"Bull! It's been my business from the beginning. Mark was my friend, and I was the first to find him after you killed him. You bet it's my business."

"Number one, Mark was never your friend, and number two, I didn't kill him, Joey did. Of course, it was under my orders." The deputy snickered again.

"Your orders? Who are you to order Mark killed, some kind of Gestapo agent?" Ed felt a hot slick of fear slide down his throat, turning into a leaden ingot in his gut. A small town upbringing had never prepared him for an encounter with a cold-blooded murderer.

"Gestapo," Longmeyer echoed. "Excellent choice of words. Yes, I ordered Mark killed. The fool tried to sharp me out of a great deal of money."

"And I suppose you killed Joey?" Ed was sweating freely now.

Longmeyer snickered. "Oh yes, I killed the traitor. He tried to back out of the Cause and I showed him the only way out."

"The Cause? What are you talking about?" Ed had never heard of any Cause club or organization in the area. The Elks and the Moose Club were in town and the Knights of Columbus at St. Bart's Church, but no Cause.

Longmeyer leaned back against the door, pointed his pistol at Ed's head and whispered, "Bang". He smiled in the darkness and educated Ed. "Let me tell you, boy. The Cause is the finest group of people who ever lived. They aren't black or red or Jews or Spics or any of those mongrel slobs out there who're always whining about equal rights, civil rights and all that other shit. They're pure white through and through and deserve to own the whole world, and we will someday, you wait and see. It's closer than you think. That goddamn Wilson thinks he can stop me and my people. He can think again. We'll be selling more than a few bags of coke through Portledge, and just maybe we'll even sell his bimbo daughter, Julie." He gurgled with demented laughter.

Ed's skin crawled as he listened to Longmeyer's tirade. He was driving a total lunatic to the farm. A short time ago the maniac had blown a hole in an old man. Now, he felt sure, the women at the farm and he were next. He had to do something to stall this guy or stop him altogether, but what? That damn gun had a madman's hand on it.

Hesitant, Ed asked, "What are you planning to do at Marlena's place? You're not going to hurt them, are you?" He could see the lights of the farmhouse and barns winking cheerfully through the trees in the distance.

"Sometimes, Eddie boy, sacrifices have to be made to make great things happen."

Ed abruptly pulled over to the side of the road. "Just what do you mean? Do you think I'm going to finish this trip so you can kill those women? Go to hell!" With those words he jerked the keys from the ignition and flung them out of the open window into the dark.

Longmeyer lunged across the seat, grabbed Ed

by the throat and jammed the pistol barrel into his ear. "You'll be real sorry you did that, you s.o.b. Now get out of the car. We'll walk the rest of the way. The deputy forced Ed out, grabbed him by the arm and pressed the gun's muzzle into his back. "Now walk real nice, Eddie, and we'll get along just fine."

One thing was for sure, Ed thought miserably, the deputy was completely nuts. In an effort to slow their progress, Ed encouraged him to talk about the Cause.

The deranged policeman responded in a ragged breath as they crossed the field rather than take a chance on being seen by passersby on the road. "What do you want to know for? You're never gonna get to join. Anyway, you're just another one of those "knee-jerk" liberals who're always crying, 'Gimme this, gimme that,' and let the government support everyone who doesn't feel like working...the welfare bums. Just get your ass in gear and don't ask any more questions." They struggled through the tall grass to reach the house.

The gravel crunched beneath Longmeyer's and Ed's shoes as they approached the kitchen door of the farmhouse. From out of the darkness several cats appeared and stroked themselves along the legs of the men.

"Get, you damn cats!" Longmeyer snarled and sent a yowling feline flying off his foot. Others took its place and within seconds several affectionate cats were milling around, causing them to slow to a shuffle.

"Knock and don't try anything funny," the deputy ordered when they reached the door. Longmeyer's pistol was still entrenched in Ed's back.

When Marlena opened the door she laughed

at the sight of two scowling men with a fluff of cats at their feet.

"What are you two up to?" Before Ed could signal any kind of warning, Longmeyer pushed him into the kitchen, knocking Marlena aside, and slammed the door shut behind him. "Deputy, are you crazy?" was all she could sputter before he pointed his .38 directly at her.

"Shut up and sit down, you fat bitch," he ordered.

Marlena put her hands to her mouth as she slowly sank onto a chair, her eyes huge. "What do you want?" she asked in a shaky voice.

"You know where Mark kept the Posse's membership lists and records. I've searched this place twice, but you've run me out both times. Now, you're gonna get them for me, and if you do it real quick, I might let you live."

"So you're in the Posse too. Mark never told me."

"There's plenty Mark never told you, you drunken slut. Now where are those records?" Longmeyer pointed the pistol menacingly.

Ed snapped, "Don't tell him anything, Mar. He'll kill both of us the minute he gets those papers. He already shot Char..." A crack across his head by the gun barrel silenced him.

"Now, Riley, aren't you just a little bit tired of headaches?" Longmeyer snickered at his own humor as blood seeped between the fingers Ed held to his gashed head.

Marlena made a move to aid Ed, but the deputy yanked her to her feet. "Find the papers, bitch, and maybe I'll let you live just to make a liar out of Riley." He grinned at Ed. "But he won't be around long enough for me to enjoy it." Holding Marlena in place with threats, he tucked his pistol into its holster, yanked Ed's arms around the chair's backrest and handcuffed him to it. He then dragged Marlena across the kitchen toward the steps leading upstairs, his fingers digging into her arm.

"Now let's find those papers," Longmeyer whispered to her in a sinister voice.

"Marlena," Ed croaked, "don't show him." He slumped forward, unconscious.

"Eddie!" she screamed and reached for him, but was stopped by Longmeyer's iron grip.

"Shut up. He ain't dead. Hurry up and get those documents."

White faced and shaking, Marlena edged her way to the second floor stairway. Longmeyer glanced at Ed, then followed closely behind her.

As soon as they were out of sight, Ed cautiously raised his head and looked around. He tried to create a plan to save Marlena and himself. First thing to do was call the cops, hopefully, honest cops. Ed stood, hunched over, the chair firmly attached to him, and shuffled over to the wall phone. He could just reach it with his mouth. He grabbed the receiver with his teeth, set it on the counter with a small clunk, and tried to dial with his nose.

"Damn," Ed complained softly. "Wish to hell she had touch tone." Every time he tried to dial the zero, it slipped off his blood-smeared nose back to its original position. He finally slumped onto the chair, exhausted.

He struggled with the handcuffs in an attempt to break the back of the chair, and was startled by faces at the window. First Annie's face, then Ben's. He could see Annie's mouth form the words, "Now what?" and they came through the door.

"What is going on?" Annie said loudly as she and Ben clattered in the door and rushed over to Ed.

"Be quiet for God's sake," Ed whispered hoarsely. "Longmeyer's upstairs with Marlena and he wants to kill us both. Get me loose and let's help Mar." But it was too late. Longmeyer, with Marlena held close to him and clutching a large business satchel to her chest, came down the steps.

"Stop right there," Longmeyer ordered. "Nobody's leaving this house." He shoved Marlena, still gripping the bag, into a nearby chair. "You two, sit down."

Ben and Annie edged around the kitchen to two free chairs at the table. Annie spoke first.

"Isn't this a nice tea party. What's next, Deputy, mass murder?"

"That's just what I have in mind horsey-girl, just what I have in mind," he replied, a death's head grin on his narrow face.

Ben spoke, "Why are you doing this, Myron? If you're going to kill us, we deserve to know the reason."

"Because I need to. I could just tie you up and go. That would give me a little head start, but I want some real leeway. Wilson may be here soon, and you'll tell him which way I went. Besides, killing you all would be a nice tidy ending to this whole 'Mark Torrence' mess. Clear the books, so to speak. But mostly I'm gonna do it because you all deserve it."

"What!?"

"What are you talking about?"

"Who the hell do you..."

"Shut up!" Longmeyer shouted. He stepped back and pointed the pistol at them with both hands. Their chorus of protests abruptly stopped. Relaxing slightly, Longmeyer looked at Ed. "You pissed me off the most. Because of Charlie's past,

I been keeping an eye on him for a long time, but you, you meddling jerk, kept talking to him until certain facts about me and my family came out. It's a good thing I followed and listened in on you two tonight. I stoppered up his yammering old mouth for good. You gave as many headaches as you got, Riley. Well, in a few minutes you won't ever have another one."

"And you, precious little Annie, everyone's darling, you were getting in the way too," Longmeyer continued. "You could probably identify pictures of people who have done a variety of business here, so I'm gonna tie up that loose end. And Ben, you're in the same boat with little Annie here. And last but not least is our favorite boozer, Marlena. You're a liability now, babe. Without Mark to keep you in booze, you might sober up into a real human being, turn on the Cause and tell Wilson everything, that uptight, upright s.o.b. Especially when you would find out Mark, aka Marco Torte of the L.A. mob, left Ben, his old cellmate, the farm, not you." He laughed at her shocked, angry expression. "That's right. He wasn't going to leave this place to a barroom pickup like you, particularly since you two weren't really married."

"So now you all know why you're going to die. Sort of like that old saying, 'curiosity killed the cat'." With that, Longmeyer pointed the pistol directly at Marlena and gently squeezed the trigger. He should have started with Ben.

Ben flipped the table at the deputy. It struck Longmeyer's arm, causing the shot to bore a beehole into the ceiling plaster.

Both Ben and Annie leaped onto Longmeyer. As they struggled to hold the thrashing deputy and scrabbled for the gun in his hand, Marlena screeched an order.

"Freeze, all of you!" She stood there, a .357 magnum pointed at the suddenly stilled group. "Sit on the floor, hands where I can see them," she ordered.

Ed, who had been clubbing Longmeyer with his chair legs, sat with a thump, his arms still firmly cuffed to the backrest. Ben and Annie slowly went into a squat, hands clearly visible on the floor. Longmeyer, still holding his gun, stiffened.

"Where'd you have the piece stashed, Marlena?" Longmeyer asked. "Up your ass?"

"Shut up, you pig!" Marlena crouched slightly and unsteadily aimed the heavy gun at them. "I got it from the drawer in the kitchen table. Now, drop that gun and get down with the rest of them."

Longmeyer slowly sank to the floor, setting his pistol within easy reach, carefully watching Marlena.

"What are you doing, Mar?" Ed asked, "We almost had him."

Marlena pointed the gun at Ed. "So what? Do you think I'm going to let all that money get away from me? There must be half a million bucks in that satchel! Wilson would just give it to the authorities and I'd be broke. No way!"

"Did you know there was money hidden in the house?" Annie asked.

"Yeah, I did, and I was going to spend it on the farm, but now that I see how much I meant to Mark, alias 'Marco', hah, screw it. I'll take the cash, instead. Now, I'm outta here, and all of you just stay down on the floor."

Clutching her pistol in one hand and hefting the heavy satchel containing the Posse records and money with the other, Marlena edged toward the door while keeping her eyes on the huddled group. As she sat the satchel down to open the door,

Longmeyer stooped and grabbed his pistol off the floor. Just as quickly, Marlena snapped off a shot. The bullet struck his neck, snapping his head backward. Fatally wounded, he collapsed to the floor.

Shocked at her own act, Marlena stiffened against the doorframe. The stunned group turned as one to stare at her. Annie, the first to react, reached out her hand to Marlena and advanced a step. "Give me the gun, Marlena."

Wildly, Marlena looked at her. "No!" she screamed, grabbed the satchel and bolted out the door.

"I'll get her," shouted Ben and scrambled after her.

The thunder of hoofbeats drowned out the slam of the screen door. The horses, panicked by the sharp gun reports, had smashed through the faulty paddock gate and stampeded down the driveway toward the house.

Annie ran out the doorway. Ed, with a desperate wrench, broke the back of the chair, partially freeing himself. He followed, his hands still cuffed behind his back and caught up with them several yards away. Lying on the driveway, was a crumpled, broken Marlena. The satchel lay nearby, clasp broken, money and papers strewn by the frantic passage of the horses that had bolted through the unmended gate.

Ben rose from Marlena's side and shook his head. "We better call an ambulance."

"Yeah," Ed replied. "Let's call Wilson, too."

Chapter 23

Within ten minutes the ambulance and every police car in the county were parked up and down the road, their lights flashing. The state and county police and Chief Wilson were standing near the kitchen door in muted conversation, while the medical examiner inspected the bodies. Yellow plastic police tape was strung around the crime scene like macabre Christmas garland. Ed, Annie and Ben huddled together off to one side of the driveway.

Wilson walked out of the house, a grim frown etching deep lines on his face, his age finally revealing itself. He approached the three of them.

"Are you people alright?"

Annie gave him a watery smile, while Ben simply shrugged his shoulders.

Wilson turned to Ed. "I see you're bleeding again."

In the dim light Ed didn't see the concern on Wilson's face; he only heard the rough tone. "Wait 'till I rub the blood from my eyes and I'll tell you about it."

"Calm down, Riley," Wilson replied, sighing. "I just want to find out why my deputy and Marlena have died. This won't be an official report, mind you. You'll give that to the county sheriff. Annie and Ben, I want you two to stay here and talk to the investigators. I'll take Ed to the ambulance for first aid. He motioned for Ed to follow him. "Come on, son. We'll get that head looked at." He walked companionably alongside Ed, who held his hand to the gash in his forehead.

As the paramedics treated Ed's wound, he related to Wilson the events that led to Longmeyer's and Marlena's deaths. Suddenly Ed remembered old Charlie. "Did anyone find Charlie at his house? Longmeyer shot him while we were there tonight."

"He's okay," Wilson replied. "The Deputy wasn't as great a marksman as he talked himself up to be, and Charlie's a tough old bird. The neighbors heard the gunshot and sent for help."

"I'm glad to hear that," Ed replied, relief flooding through him.

"Chief," Ed asked, "what was the 'Cause' that Longmeyer raved about? Are they the same bunch we encountered at Miller's farm? Sounded like a bunch of anarchists to me."

Wilson, face grim, shook his head. "The group is called 'Posse Comitatus.' And you're right, they are one in the same. They think the county government is the highest in the country, the county sheriff is the only legal law enforcement officer in the United States and the members of the Posse will enforce the "law" if the sheriff won't. They've had shootouts with federal law enforcement officers. Many won't pay income tax and that's barely scratching the surface. It's another crazy fringe bunch, and from what our investigation has found, Longmeyer, Mark, Marlena and Lorenzo were all members, Longmeyer being the leader. The men were dealing drugs to support the non-working members and to pay for assult weapons. They kept

Marlena somewhat in the dark because of her drinking. Myron Longmeyer knew we were closing in on him, so he made a desperate attempt to eliminate witnesses before he escaped. We were going to arrest him tonight."

Ed shook his head slowly. "So that's what all the police were doing in town tonight. Boy, have I been blind. I never dreamed something like that was going on around here. Mark was always so nice to me. Kind of makes you wonder who to trust."

"It's over now. You can win a writing prize with it and be Portledge's famous son." Wilson gave Ed a quick, almost friendly smile and joined some other police on the scene.

Ed looked up to see Pollard approaching, barge-like, toward him. Oh God, thought Ed, not another ration of shit.

"I see you're still living," Pollard observed.

"You disappointed?" Ed replied.

"Naw, you little twit." Pollard gave him an almost comradely cuff. "We may butt heads, kid, but it's kinda fun. If you'd gotten killed think of all the entertainment I'd miss. Besides, watching you in action is better than a Stooges film. See you on the next case, kid." He laughed and waddled off officiously.

Mute with surprise, Ed watched him leave, wondering, am I a bad judge of character or is he a split personality? Finished at the ambulance, Ed joined Ben and Annie, who had been questioned by Wilson and dismissed for the time being. They gathered the now tired horses and locked them in their stalls, then gravitated to Annie's cottage to talk.

"The first thing I want to know is how those horses got out?" Ed demanded as they sat down in the minuscule kitchen.

"That was my fault," replied Ben. "I never mended the paddock gate latch and I guess the shot that killed Longmeyer set them off. By the time Marlena ran from the house they were running full tilt by the door. She got in their way."

Annie placed cans of pop on the table and sat down. She glared at Ben and snapped the pop-tops like pistol shots, then shoved one in front of him. "I want to know what you were in prison for."

"Aw, Annie. It wasn't much. I was just a smartass kid helping Mark...Marco, run some numbers in L.A. and we got caught. Fortunately, we ended up in the same prison and Mark kept the men from giving me a hard time, if you get my drift." Ben laughed wryly. "He told them I was his boyfriend, and if they bothered me, he'd have them killed. He made sure they knew about his mob connections."

"Nobody gets away from the mob, I've heard," added Ed. "How did you two do it?"

"Luckily, we both got out the same day, and literally snuck out of town. Then we thumbed across the country until we got in Ohio and believe it or not, we really did win a big lottery. We each chipped in ten bucks to buy a bunch of tickets, and damned if we didn't hit it for a hundred grand." Ben slapped the table with glee, but immediately frowned. "Too bad the son-of-a-bitch cheated me."

Annie, sitting next to Ben, placed her hand near his and asked, "How so?"

Ben's face twisted into a scowl. "That night, while we were celebrating, he met Marlena. Man, what a babe she was then. He got drunk and spent the night with her. Next thing I knew, she was traveling with us to Pennsylvania, and Mark bought the farm, with her in the house and me in the shack out back. I trusted him with the winnings and he put the place in his name alone. I was young and dumb. I was just grateful to have a little place of my own. Funny how it all turned out, huh?" Dry from the long speech, he took a deep swig from the can.

Astonished, Annie stared at Ben and said, "That's some story. Is that all there is? Shiny-suited men with sinister faces aren't going to show up here some day and gun you down, are they?"

Ben smiled apologetically at her. "No. Even though we wriggled out like little scared snakes, the people from the west coast had no interest in us. Small fish, ya know? We're in the clear."

The skepticism cleared from her face to be replaced by relief. "This has been one lulu of a mess, hasn't it?" she said. "I thought Mark was such a great guy. And poor Marlena. What a way to go. The very animals she hated did her in. Ironic, isn't it?"

"Yeah, she was getting her life back on track. No drinking or screaming at whoever came along," added Ed. "By the way, Ben. Where were you the other night after you got out of the slammer? It made you look like your basic suspicious character."

"I was earning points, Eddie. The county sheriff and Chief Wilson were getting an earful just about the time Annie's cat was using you for a scratching post." Ben glanced at Annie and they both laughed.

"I'm glad you two find my pain so amusing," Ed said sourly. "What are you two going to do now with both Marlena and Mark gone? It's a big place to work shorthanded, Ben."

"I'd like to operate it," Ben quickly answered, "but I need a partner." He looked directly and expectantly at Annie, grasped her hand and smiled warmly.

She smiled back, and a strong blush basted her face. "Okay, okay, I'll give it serious consideration, since things have changed." She responded to the surprise on Ed's face. "Ben and I have been seeing each other on the Q.T. for a while now. We weren't too sure how Mark and Marlena would react to us as a couple. Especially Mark. He was such a control freak, there was no telling what he might do."

Ben added, "And Annie and I had been talking to Marlena about a three way partnership the last few days, but we weren't too crazy about having her as a business partner. Too unpredictable. I guess now it's a moot point." He kissed Annie's hand, still held fast in his grip. "But it will be our place now."

Then Annie, smiling suggestively at Ben and pleading exhaustion, kicked Ed out.

Ed's hope of a romance deflated, he scuffed down the driveway thinking about Annie and Ben. Brother, what a waste of perfectly good fantasies, he groused silently.

The crime lab people were still working at the farmhouse, but things were a lot quieter than earlier.

Ed paused to watch the last ambulance taking Marlena away. The cold, damp night air seeped through his clothes and he felt a loneliness settle over him. He'd miss Marlena and Mark. The two of them were such a colorful pair that their absence would make life a lot less interesting. It brought to mind other people who made his life more interesting and he resolved to visit Charlie at the hospital the next day. Now he could make sure Charlie got the proper recognition for his heroism and help the old guy clear his name once and for all. After that he'd check in on his mother. She might need a wall washed or something.

Walking along the road, he thought out how to write the final story of Mark and Marlena, Joey and the lawless Deputy Longmeyer. He thought of Ted Russell and smiled grimly at the stink Ted would raise at being left out of the final story. Live with it, Ted.

Ed fished his spare ignition key from his pocket and walked down the road to his car. The lights from the parked police cruisers bathed his path blood red.

Chapter 24

Ed flicked on the light at his desk. Its reflection on the window panes blotted out the streetlit scene outside, creating a small movie screen on which the bizarre events of the past several days replayed themselves.

The image of the slumped form of Mark, a steak knife protruding from his abdomen, flickered like a vintage film. Why, Ed wondered, did a man who had served his time and managed to escape the long arm of the Mafia want to climb into the snakepit of drug dealing? Easy money? Hah! Easy death or another stretch in jail was more like it. That group, the Posse, wasn't worth the price Mark had paid.

Lorenzo's screen time played like a popular slasher movie. The grisly scene still made Ed shudder. Slumped in his kitchen, his neck brutally sliced open by a maniac wielding a steak knife, Joey had paid a huge price for his involvement with Myron Longmeyer. All Joey's wild living had culminated in an equally wild death.

All the stampede scenes in the old western movies he had watched on T.V. as a kid galloped across his window and he could see Marlena under the hooves of all those crazed horses. She was working so hard at turning over the proverbial "new leaf". The shock of Ben inheriting the farm had caused her to fling the damn leaf down, grab the money and run. At least she had tried to run. The terrified horse, Rita, and her thundering herd put a stop to that almost instantly.

Ah, the romantic part. Ed and Annie. Oops, sorry. Annie and Ben. A brief moment of them kissing each other flashed, but Ed squeezed his eyes shut and blotted out the sight. "I don't know what she sees in him," he muttered. "He's got to be in his thirties. Way too old for a girl in her twenties." He determinedly shook thoughts of her from his mind. "Plenty more where she came from," he muttered.

Satisfaction wreathed Ed's face when the window screen seemed to enlarge featuring Charlie, in his World War II uniform, riding in a convertible with the top down being doused by ticker tape in a parade in his honor. This scene, vowed Ed, would be a reality if he had anything to say about it. He would fight the government, the Army, Longmeyer's relatives and anyone else who tried to keep him from clearing Charlie Smith's name. Ed was very glad Charlie would live to enjoy it.

After the vignettes had played themselves out, Ed began typing his report on his old machine, dabbing out his many errors with whiteout. He wrote up Longmeyer's and Marlena's deaths as a separate story, but wrote another one describing entire the sequence of events that began with the murder of Mark and ended with Marlena's accidental death. He carefully included his own involvement every step of the way. If a big paper picked this up, he considered, he wanted them to know he knew how to cover a story until it was finished. Mac may not want to print this, Ed thought, but you never know. It would look great below the fold on page one.

Ed stacked the smudgy papers off to one side, pushed the typewriter away and turned off the light. According to his watch, Ed hoped tiredly, the sky in the east would soon lighten into a death-free day. He rubbed his gritty eyes and yawned, then rested his head in his arms on the desk and slept.

Once again, Ed was jostled awake by Mac. "Hey, Ed, don't you have a home?" Mac asked as he gently shook Ed by the arm. Mac picked up the stacked copy from the corner of the desk and inquired as Ed stretched and yawned, "What's this? More midnight mayhem?"

Ed watched with sleepy satisfaction as Mac's eyes widened at the content of Ed's report.

With the story crumpled in his fist, Mac eyed Ed, a look of disbelief on his broad face. "A dead deputy sheriff, a stampeded woman and a gunned down old man. Quite a story. Did this really happen or have you embellished this just a tad?"

"I wish it was an embellishment," Ed replied with a fizz of anger, "but go ahead, call Wilson, call the county cops. They'll tell you the same story. Longmeyer murdered Joey and he shot Charlie Smith, Marlena killed Longmeyer and the horses galloped over Mar when she ran off. It was quite a party. You should have been there."

"Been years since I did hard news. I don't know if my heart could take it," Mac replied, smiling.

From across the room at the entry door a clipped voice cut into their conversation. "Sleeping on the job again, Riley. Seems like Mac's waking you up on a pretty regular basis." Ted Russell blew in the room flapping a handful of papers at them. "Read 'em and weep, Riley. I've scooped you on the wrap up of the Torrence affair." Russell handed Mac the crisp sheets and stood, arms crossed on his chest, with a proud expression on his face.

Mac glanced briefly at Ed and then started reading. After finishing the article he said. "I'm sorry, Ted. I can't use it. I have an eyewitness report and it's already been turned in."

"What? How can that be?" Ted blustered. "I just got this from a county policeman who had been at Torrences'. He hadn't been back in his office two minutes when I talked to him." Suddenly Ted's eyes riveted on Ed's broadly grinning face. "You, again?" he burst out, enraged.

"Me, again," replied Ed, and beamed up at his infuriated colleague. He was completely unprepared for Ted's next move.

Ted reached out and grabbed the papers from Mac's hand and before Ed or Mac could stop him, he ripped the story into several hundred ragged-edged flakes and flung them up into the air. "Now try to print it, Riley," he snapped as the paper snowstorm fluttered to the floor around them. "After you finally tape it back together, it'll be old news."

Ed leaped from his chair to grab Ted. "What the hell! Are you nuts?"

Mac pushed Ed back into his seat with one hand and grabbed Ted's arm with the other and walked him a few steps away from Ed's desk. "Hey, Ted. The kid got the story fair and square. There's no need for you to go bananas over it."

"The Torrence story was mine, damn it. Why should a kid like Riley cash in on the hottest news to hit this town in years?" Ted scowled over his shoulder at Ed.

"Because he was on the scene first, Ted. When

you're on the scene first you'll scoop him. Now I don't want to hear another word about this, you got it?" Mac immediately turned back to Ed and picked up the remaining report.

As they watched Ted slam from the room, Ed asked, "That was his own story he demolished, wasn't it?"

"Yeah," Mac replied, shaking his head, "but he must have thought it was yours. I'm going to give him a week off without pay for that little trick."

"Is that all?" Ed asked in surprise. Yanking a finished story from the boss's hand and destroying it seemed like it deserved worse punishment than that. If he had done it, Mac probably would have fired him.

"For Ted, yes. He's earned a little leeway for his hard work over the years. If you had done it, I'd have fired your ass." Mac then returned to his office, dropping both of Ed's reports into the story box on the secretary's desk on the way by.

Ed sagged tiredly in his chair as other employees entered the room, styrofoam cups of steaming coffee in hand. He flipped them a group wave.

"Hey, Eddie. Having a sleepover again?"

"Whatsa matter, Riley? Landlord lock you out?"

Marge approached Ed, a concerned light in her eyes. "Are you all right, Eddie? Witnessing the death of Deputy Longmeyer and Mrs. Torrence must have been horrible for you."

"You must have a grapevine that would blanket Brazil, Marge," Ed replied, lightly. He still wasn't sure how he felt about the previous evening, and wasn't going to string some line of bull. Mostly, he felt numb.

She patted his arm lightly as if she understood, smiled reassuringly and returned to her desk. It left more space for the others to pack in around him to pump for more information.

"Listen, you guys. It'll all be in today's edition. The whole damn story from beginning to end, so you can read all about it then. I'm going home now. It's been too long a night." Ed worked his way through the disappointed group, loped down the steps and left the building.

Ed stood at the top of the steps and sucked in a lungful of cool morning air as he gazed up and down the familiar main street of Portledge. The storefronts with their awnings rolled up and still dark because of the early hour, stared back with blank eyes as though they were just waking and hadn't yet gathered their thoughts. I wonder if Annie or Ben would take me on as a riding student, he thought idly. It's been a long time since I've sat a horse. A kind of healing began as Ed trotted lightly down the steps.

About The Author

Mickey Scheuring, born and raised in Chenango County, New York, received her college degree at State University of New York at Delhi in the Animal Science program. She now resides in the Pittsburgh, Pa. area with her husband and two children.

In the past she has worked as a lab technician in pharmacology, endocrinology, and pharmaceuticals.

Now, Mickey has expanded into the writing field with the Eddie Riley mystery series. She finds the escape into the world of her hero, Eddie, the brash young newsman, a refreshing alternative to her daily life.